FLIGHT OF MAN
Tales of spirit, determination and the challenges of life on the red planet!

A trilogy set on Mars in the twenty-third Earth century... if Earth had survived.

Book One
THE EDEN SOLDIERS

Book Two
SATURN'S VANGUARD

Book Three
THE SOL REUNION

ABOUT THE AUTHOR
Canadian writer and author, Andrew Bell was born and bred in the shadows of the Rocky Mountains. His strong and active imagination has resulted in the trilogy – Flight of Man – novels of life and challenges on Mars. The Eden Soldiers, the first book in the series, is set in the year 2251. With writing now occupying his life, he continues to live in Alberta with wife Kristine.

Copyright © 2012 Andrew Bell
The right of Andrew Bell to be identified as the Author of the Work
has been asserted by him in accordance with the
Copyright, Designs and Patent Act 1988.

Published in the United States by
CUSTOM BOOK PUBLICATIONS

ISBN978-1-4792-4059-3
ISN10 1479240591

All the characters are fictitious and any resemblance to real persons,
living or dead, is purely coincidental.

TYPESET in Times New Roman 12pt
COVER PHOTOGRAPH Mars ...NASA 2011-12

FLIGHT OF MAN

THE EDEN SOLDIERS
by Andrew Bell

Book One of a Trilogy

To: Mom
Your support is beyond special.

Andrew Bell.

CHAPTER I
Wednesday, 17 March, 2251

The sun, Sol, has been protecting mankind for thousands of years and the solar system for millions beyond that. Even on that day thirty-five years ago, Sol reached out to save what child planets it could from an attack beyond imagination. A star, Bane, tore into our backyard bent on snuffing out all traces of our people.

We all knew that Bane's henchmen planets would ultimately destroy our Earth but it was Sol that grabbed onto Bane and pulled it away from its murderous rampage to spare Mars. The two giants battle in the sky above and it is now that we give thanks to our protective star. That marvellous ball of gas did what no god has done... actually stepped up to the plate and saved our tiny butts!

To punctuate the point the sun made its appearance through the light green-grey of the planetary haze now surrounding Mars. The tiny yellow light triggered some of the crystal fragments that hung in the air, creating a trail of sparks along the beams that cut their way down to the surface. It gave a stark contrast to the steely grey of the fortress. The effect only lasted a few moments but it was what the group had come to see.

The troopers applauded the speech given by the young Warrant Officer though it was not really part of the sun ceremony. Several troopers smiled at the attempt and there were a few laughs for the little fellow. The dozen or so men and women in combat armour making up the group plus a few more workers in civilian pressure suits had all stood on the south-eastern section of the wall on this morning. They all made a point of shaking the hand of their speech master.

'Well put, Bill,' a tech in a civilian environmental suit said.

'Outside the fort, its Buzz,' Buzz smiled and shook the man's hand.

'A bit dramatic, wasn't it?' Buzz's CO, TJ commented although he still wore a smile. 'We should be getting back down. Once First Recon finishes drill we'll be on deck.'

'You know one day they're going to ask you to run one of these,' Buzz fell into step with Lieutenant T.J. Marso on the way back down through a comfortably wide tunnel heading to the south barracks inside the fort. Clearly energized by the event, he was almost skipping inside his armour, fully living up to his call-sign.

In just two hours and six minutes, Bane, the star of destruction, the killer star, would also rise and chase Sol across the Martian sky. Its daily climb in the sky was never celebrated, never cherished, never intentionally watched.

Fort Grey was little more than what its name implied. It was essentially just a lookout post roughly fifteen hundred feet in diameter. A central structure in the shape of a hollowed out four-point star, dominated the area from the middle of a small clustering of buildings. Its exterior grey granite walls were sloped at forty-five degrees to deflect the heavy winds blowing to and from the coast, which lay thirty miles due south at its nearest point.

The smaller structures clustered around the massive twelve-foot high walls of the fortress were home to some local farmers and a couple adventurous entrepreneurs. Their buildings had sloped walls as well, though not nearly to the degree as those of the fort. All the cluster buildings were designed as odd shaped doughnuts with all the living and working quarters ringing a central compound and a vehicle bay for one or two ground vehicles. Large domes covered the interior yards of every building, from the little work huts to the mighty fort itself. These covered areas allowed the inhabitants to pursue daily life in a properly filtered atmosphere that was optimized for maximum oxygen and minimal particle content and all without the use of the power armour.

Even though sunrise had only just arrived at Fort Grey, ending nearly thirteen hours of darkness and beginning yet another seven hours of daylight in the twenty-hour Martian day, the Eden Peninsula Rim Station was bursting with activity.

The Eden Peninsula was the only portion of Mars that was currently inhabited by humans even after more than fifty years of occupation. It was the section chosen to test the terraforming process on Earth's first colony. While the majority of the surface was still red with Martian soil and the deep purple colouring of the oceans, the peninsula had a lush biosphere created primarily by the Terran scientists and a little Martian nature influence. Once the habitat had stabilized the Terran government had sent out the *okay* for colonization.

Since the destruction of the solar system years ago, there have been little or no altercations in which any of the two hundred thousand precious human lives on Mars had been lost. But on this day in late March, just three hours prior to the rise of Sol, a military transport convoy consisting of twelve men and women from the southern city of Fort Saturn, disappeared while en route to the northern city of New Venus. Though reports of the incident were sketchy at best, the one thing known for certain was that almost all contact with the group had been lost.

A search and rescue team dispatched from the regional capital had located a dazed and battered man ten miles southeast of the city and just short of the point where contact was lost. The man's environmental armour was in such bad shape, it was not even worth the time or energy to repair it. The man claimed to be the sole survivor of the lost transport convoy, although no record could be found to corroborate his claim.

His story, included within a priority report transmitted to the Fort Grey base commander, stated that *large flying men in armour* had attacked and destroyed the lead convoy transport prior to his abrupt evacuation. Nothing to indicate the supposed transport destruction or that of any other part of the convoy could be found within the fifty miles search grid of the direction the convoy had taken. This obviously cast a shadow of doubt on the apparent survivor's story.

Being nearly two hundred miles south-southeast from the of Fort Saturn, Fort Grey was the southern-most settlement on the Eden Peninsula which meant the militia commander had to have all his personnel on a Level Two Alert to be ready for a search mission. Whilst a formality this still meant the watch had to be doubled in size. Meanwhile, the base commander read the report again with great interest.

*When the side of the transport ripped open I knew we were done for. I had stowed away in the cargo hold of the BRAT for a free ride to the outer cities not die at the hands of some **large flying men in armour**. I just started yelling but the crew seemed to have concerns other than some freeloader.*

'They're coming through!' I yelled to no one in particular.

'Who said that?' a female voice yelled back from the control cabin.

'Forget him, watch out for those, those things!' a male voice said.

'Sol won't protect us this time,' replied another man I could not see.
'To hell with Sol!' the woman screamed as the glass shattered in the forward compartment.

That is when I felt the vehicle start to turn then flip violently to the side. The force threw me to the wall in the blink of an eye but there was no wall there. Those things outside had ripped it open seconds before so I was flying through the air in the middle of both a battle and a heavy storm. The wind grabbed me the second I was clear of the BRAT Transport and tossed me back over the hill we had just come over.
When I looked back I saw armoured men flying around the transport as I sailed through the air. The moment I hit the ground my memory for the day ended. The next memory was that of the rescue team from Fort Saturn reviving me. I saw no sign of the transport I was riding or the cargo I had hidden in.'

One hour after sunrise, D100 hours that day, Commander Martel was in his corner office at the southern end of Fort Grey taking a final look over of the report of the survivor's ordeal. Martel, a stocky man in his late forties by Earth years, was old enough to clearly remember the lights in the sky that fateful day long ago when the Earth was destroyed. His round face was worn by too many unpleasant surprises but his grey eyes still shone with the fire of youth. He was heavy-set and balding but did not mind either condition.

Commander Martel was one of the few career military officers without the hardened heart of one turned sour by frustration and arrogance. He had the mental abilities of the wisest of the top brass, even more so. Laughter came easily to this little man, which had only added to the respect he had earned during his career.

He reflected on the report, realizing the first thing making this person's story hard to believe was that in all the years living with this new atmosphere, it was a well-known fact air travel at any altitude of less than two thousand feet was all but impossible. The gas planet's intervention with the terraforming process in the first year of the New Earth Calendar had seen to that.

The atmosphere obstructing line of unassisted sight further than a single mile from even the tallest mountains in the area, was also responsible for preventing air travel. With dust and fragments of *Paernas* crystals constantly hanging in the air, a flier just could not punch through the particle rich haze fast enough to gain lift let alone rapid movement. All the aircraft that had tried travelling faster than forty-five miles-per-hour were quickly shredded into thousands of pieces. This was one of the reasons why the councils for the Eden colony had always opted to use hovercraft over-air vehicles.

The winds on the peninsula also played a major part in the council's decision. The average windstorm would last as little as an hour, but consisted of winds in excess of one-hundred and fifty mph. Because Mars was smaller than Earth had been, it had a lighter gravitational pull even with the core of the gas giant buried deep inside –the same core that had crashed into the planet at the moment the Earth was destroyed. This meant even in the lightest of storms people had been swept as far as ten miles away. Even the powerful hover vehicles the council cherished so much, had to secure themselves to the ground as best they could in the event a storm caught them away from the protective walls of a garage. With all these factors against the development of personal flying armour, it seemed next to impossible the survivor saw any such units.

Second and more importantly, the Search and Rescue team from Fort Saturn found no physical wreckage. Only several scrape marks were found at the farthest edge of the search pattern indicating a hover vehicle of some kind was running disabled, though the age of the mark was in dispute. The survivor's report indicated there had been a severe windstorm at the time of the attack. He claimed the high winds had pushed the engagement in a southerly direction and after he had been thrown clear a crosswind caught him and threw him northwards. Though such events were not entirely unheard of, the likelihood of it happening in a major storm was extremely doubtful.

Indeed, the marks on the ground showed that something went south from the scene of the supposed *battle* but there was still no proof it was the missing convoy. Regardless of what had made those marks, it had happened in Fort Grey's area of influence, and it was up to Commander Martel to determine the validity of the report, in whole or in part.

Few things like this ever happened to Base Commander Martel, not since the early days when people went crazy with grief and started looting anything and everything, and he dreaded every instance when it happened. His job at this point was as clear as a crystal shard and just as pleasant as swallowing one. He had to choose a squad of his own men and women to investigate this problem, on the off chance that there was some truth to the survivor's claims.

The last time he had sent a squad on a mission half as uncertain as this one there had been an accident where two of his men were lost. It was a part of the job but that did not mean he had to enjoy it. He believed the ideal situation was when a base commander had the same people under his or her command when he or she left as when they had taken the post, except for those drummed out or retired. He tortured himself for nearly a week afterwards and, in fact, still harboured some ill feelings for having let it happen.

His office was large for an outpost office spreading thirty feet across and giving him enough room for a large desk. It was a warm and inviting room that everyone felt comfortable in most days but he did not want to be here today.

'Amanda,' he said as he placed the report back in the brown folder in which it had arrived and flopped it down on his otherwise barren desk, 'get me the squad leader currently on active standby.'

'Yes sir,' the young woman replied. She had been standing patiently on the far side of the Commander's desk while he read and now clipped out a crisp salute in proper military fashion. Her auburn hair whipped around as she spun on her heels and marched out of the office. Her crisp boot steps echoed through the halls of the command bunker as if she were on parade. Outside she adjusted her crisp uniform to better suit her slender frame before she walked out of the commander's bunker.

Major Amanda Harte was not exactly a towering figure at only five-foot-nine but she carried an air of confidence beyond her rank that seemed to shrink almost everyone else. She came from a long line of fine military officers, which could undoubtedly be traced as far back as the old Terran days, though genealogy records of that time had been lost. However, her family was noted in military records as far back as 2150 Old Earth calendar. While these records allowed her to follow her heritage, there was not much detail as to who these men and women were.

At twenty-three, she was probably the youngest woman to have ever made the rank of Major, and definitely the youngest person to be promoted to the position of second in command of a major military installation.

Just past the outer wall of the command bunker she paused to don her uniform jacket, which she had removed as part of a new protocol being implemented to deter pirates from smuggling weapons in or out. Pirates were not a major problem anymore but the brass thought it would be best to take the extra step so as to not make it too easy for them.

She stepped out into a wide *outside* walkway, sheltered by the protective dome, and purposefully made her way towards the training compound at the centre of the fort. There were no plants or flowers along this twelve foot wide walkway, no color deviance from the steel grey of the walls aside from the red rock of the path and uniforms of the techs and troopers. This was a militia base and in her mind that was the way it should be. There should be nothing to distract from the missions given out by a superior officer, like her. Ordinarily she would not need her jacket under the dome but as she entered the fringe of the compound the air suddenly got much cooler, which was an odd occurrence though not uncommon.

Sunlight trickled through the dome into an area almost a hundred yards across. Again there was only the red of the stone flooring to off-set the walls. Somehow the red seemed to glow when the sunlight finally reached it. The reason for the temperature difference was obvious as she stepped into the main training arena. There was a squad performing exercises and the low temperature kept the troops cooler, thus increasing the amount of time spent in training. These troops were not training in their power armour as may have been expected. The armour was designed so the natural movement of a trooper would not be hindered by anything, including the atmosphere and the bulk of the armour itself ... any training here would translate easily.

In additional to the jacket rule the Eden Council had decided in Year 2 NEC - New Earth Calendar – that the wearing of power-assisted armour within the pressurized facility was prohibited as it made the citizens feel uncomfortable. They even passed a law to support their ruling. She hated curbing military needs for civilian comfort.

Major Harte strode clear of the south barracks heading towards the exercise compound at the centre of the fort.

Her passage would cause both civilians and soldiers alike to pause in their activities to stand at attention. She provided a crisp return salute to the troops, which each of them probably deserved though she had not run any ops with any of them. Amanda enjoyed the unconditional respect she was shown wherever she went, whether inside or outside of Fort Grey.

Her barely concealed joy and pride stuttered and collapsed, however, when her eyes came upon an officer leaning casually against the corner of the western bank of the south barracks. He was a taller man, perhaps six foot give or take a couple of inches, with a strong and well-defined build. His dark hair was cropped short, no more than a half an inch in length. The grey in his eyes seemed almost to glow a kind of silver as he spoke. As always, his uniform was crisp and in perfect condition even after attending one of those stupid ceremonies – oddly enough, it even looked good while he was standing in the half-slouch position he was currently in.

He was Lieutenant Trevor James Marso, or TJ as everyone called him, the commanding officer of Fort Grey's Second Recon Squad. A man of several years of field experience, he was well liked among the stationed troops. The wiry young Warrant Officer standing beside TJ visibly shook in his rigid attention as Amanda's eyes turned to glacier ice yet still managed to burn as she glared at the slouching officer. TJ was busy fussing with a thread that had worked itself loose and therefore had not seen the approach of the Fort's Second Officer. Whether that would have made a difference or not who could say.

Everyone called the Warrant Officer by his call sign of Buzz though his real name was Bill Zedluk. He was the embodiment of the ninety-eight pound weakling. No one knows how he got into the militia being as small as he was but he remained very popular so no one seemed to mind. His blond hair was cut short but always seemed to stick straight up like he had just stuck his finger in an electrical outlet.

'On your feet there, sir,' whispered the young soldier.

TJ looked up at the young man and then over to Amanda Harte, 'Relax Bill,' he smiled, 'I see her, besides she's mostly a steam-powered android, anyway.'

If a person could actually die from a look, TJ would have been no more than a cloud of dust at this moment. But before things got too out of control and overheated, as they tended to get with these two, he snapped to a formal parade attention and gave the proper snap salute to his superior officer and patiently awaited the correct response.

Amanda was not impressed with this display and gave TJ a quick, haughty sniff and a quicker salute. She then turned away sharply and headed the rest of the way into the training compound at a brisk march.

'See there Bill, she blew an O-ring at the end there,' TJ laughed with a throaty chuckle once the major was out of earshot.

'You should watch yourself around that one, chief. I hear she's out gunning for you,' replied Buzz, a little quieter than he needed.

'What's she going to do, Buzz? Send me to Earth?' He laughed again.

'I wouldn't put it past her.' He eyed the major carefully to ensure he had not been heard.

Amanda was furious! The bastard had absolutely no respect for authority, or at the very least for her. That thought, and in particular the latter half of it, almost had her fuming enough to storm back to the slouching, insolent prick and punch his lights out. In fact, she was about to turn around when she saw the original object of her journey through the *openair* of Fort Grey.

She was a pretty woman with long blond hair coming down to her waist. Her body was not large, but it was well built. Standing a full five inches shorter than Amanda she emitted a meek aura, though she was anything but. Lieutenant Daniella Klon was the squad leader for the First Recon Squad, the current standby squad.

She was putting a new recruit through his paces with live blades when Amanda approached the pair. She knew they were live weapons thanks to her own training and waited well out of range. The rest of the squad was training with the safety weapons differentiated by their color, green for live and red for safe – a somewhat counter intuitive arrangement but the crystals that gave the blades their cutting power only came in green. The recruit was new even to Amanda's eyes but he was good enough with the equipment to hold off the Lieutenant's attacks, although he was not perfect by the looks of his skirmish outfit.

As Amanda stepped up to the slightly raised training platform Lieutenant Klon and her recruit-in-training finished their scrimmage and deactivated their potentially lethal weapons. Now she could get a good look at the young private, who she now recognized only as Erik something-or-other, she could see he had three severe slashes and some minor cuts about his body and was listing to one side, clutching at a particularly nasty slice near his hip.

Erik was a large fellow who literally towered over Daniella in all dimensions. He had a heavy build consisting of muscle with little fat but nonetheless far from a sculpted form. His head was completely bald by his own hand; his dark goatee the only indication of what his hair would look like.

'Your uniform is a total mess and unbecoming of a trooper of the Militia. Get those wounds tended to and a new uniform then report back to your barracks, Private,' Amanda ordered with all the authority she could muster though her smile.

'Yes ma'am,' Erik barked through a wince and limped off towards the medical bunker at the west end of the fort at the best speed he could gather.

The two women watched as he unsteadily made his way out of earshot. 'You could go a little easier on him, especially after what I just finished doing to him,' Daniella smiled.

'I guess, but sometimes it's fun to see them squirm a little.'

'So then, what's so darned important that makes you interrupt my exercises?'

'Oh yeah. Thanks for reminding me; I've got a recon romp through the countryside for your squad. Well it's more like wreckage sifting now that I think of it.' Her smile widened.

'Oh goody!' Daniella muttered with a half-smile and a roll of the eyes. 'What is it this time, if I may ask? Some drunken convoy drivers lose their radar dish again? Or my favourite ...somebody's helmet has flown off their rock-filled head and little ol' me has to go pick it up.'

'Not a hundred percent sure on this one. You've got to come with me to the Commander's office. He is going to explain it.' Amanda's smile was gone, replaced by her business face.

'Sounds serious, Amanda,' she said, her smile now gone too. The women started towards the command bunker as they talked.

'Could be,' Major Harte paused and glared off ahead of them at the two men still standing against the wall. 'Doesn't that man ever work? There is tons of work to be done, almost literally.'

'Who?' Daniella whirled around to look in the direction that Amanda was staring in and saw TJ laughing it up with Buzz as now a few others of his squad joined them.

'Oh, hey, listen Amanda; don't pay too much attention to him. It just encourages him, he is kind of cute though,' she added.

'Hey now, he's the enemy here, sweetheart; don't go soft on me,' Amanda joked.

'Not the enemy from where I'm standing, sister,' she laughed. She shifted her eyes back to Amanda, 'Anyway, just ignore him, dear.'

'I know, but he knows exactly where and how to push me. If only I could fire his butt out of one of our beam cannons, I'd be so much happier!'

The two women exchanged a glance and burst out laughing as they walked to the command bunker. The soldiers Amanda had passed on the way out to get Daniella now stopped and looked after their Major in bewilderment at the uncommon emotion being displayed.

*****

CHAPTER II
Later, Wednesday, 17 March, 2251

Commander Martel stood with his back to the two women still standing at attention as he contemplated how to give the order. He was trying again to justify the whole situation to himself. He had spent the last hour outlining the area to be searched, the details of the convoy's cargo manifest and going over what had happened since the convoy had gone missing. All that remained was to explain to the squad leader why this mission was to be carried out.

'Ladies,' he began as he turned to face them. The air was stale in his office adding to his tensions and all but broadcasting to these women that he had not been out in a long time, 'this is a sensitive incident and would normally be handled by a much larger installation than us, like Fort Saturn. But because of the nature of the cargo all speed possible is necessary. The windstorm that supposedly rattled the convoy during... whatever happened out there... is still registering on our weather tracking system. This means it could still be pushing the convoy in our direction at some twenty-five miles-per-hour. That alone means units from this base will be able to intercept whatever is left far quicker than units from Fort Saturn.'

'But sir,' Daniella interrupted, 'the search area you've laid out for us is huge! How do you expect us to find a single convoy out there, even if anything is left? Besides, it is going to be well after dark before we get there. Even if we do have a GCR, it'll take us three days if we're lucky.'

'I can appreciate that, Lieutenant, and that is why I'm giving you a second Ground Car. Take your entire squad so that the actual search doesn't take so long.'

'Two GCRs and the whole squad? It's that dangerous?'

'No, no, it's not. Just that,' he paused a moment. He did not want the women to notice his nervousness and apprehension about the mission, 'you'll need more eyes and personal sensor units so you're not gone for days on end, remember?'

'Yeah, you've got a point there. I don't like it though,' Daniella sighed.

'It's settled; assemble your people and be ready to leave in two hours' time.'

'Yes, sir,' she saluted.

The compound seemed to explode into activity not more than thirty seconds after Lieutenant Klon emerged from the Base Commander's office. Orders were barked left and right sending men and women scurrying to and from every possible corner of the fort. Two techs, who had been performing routine maintenance around the medical bunker before any of the orders came down, snapped their heads around when the shouts for vehicles began and bolted clear across three-hundred feet of the training ground of the fort to the vehicle bay to begin prepping the GCRs for their mission. Not far behind them emerged the young private, fully regenerated though still stiff. He heard the orders being called out and knew the time for action was here, got caught up in the excitement and ran to the north barracks to ready his gear for what he heard the seasoned soldiers were predicting would be a dull assignment. But it was to be his first time out and the excitement had him strung so tight you could have bounced a quarter off his chest.

'Geez, this is nuts,' Erik shouted above the racket. 'Is it always like this before a mission?'

'Nope,' replied another private by the name of Martin, 'only when the directive comes down with less than a day to prepare. Most of the time it's a little less screwed up.'

'Why so short a time, do you think?' he asked while slipping into his power armour

'Don't know. Rumour has it there was a meteor strike not too far off.'

'They're sending us out in full force for a meteor hit? That doesn't sound right,' he said.

'It's the top brass, man, what do you expect?' Martin laughed.

Not more than seventy minutes passed before Daniella's squad was assembled at the southwest gate in their full power armour and outfitted with maximum firepower. Commander Martel came up from his office to give the troopers the once-over before sending them beyond the walls. He walked down the line of troopers and around both of the GCRs and nodded at each.

'Everyone and everything looks to be in order, Lieutenant,' Commander Martel said above the fading racket. 'You may proceed with your assignment at your discretion.' He promptly turned away. He never liked to watch his troops head out in case they never made it home again.

Ninety minutes after the order was given, all supplies and equipment were loaded into the waiting cargo compartments of the GCRs and the squad moved past Fort Grey's sloped walls. They proceeded on a northwest course to intercept the supposedly crippled convoy and salvage whatever they could, if there was anything out there at all. Though Commander Martel could not see over the walls from his office, he stared at where he knew he would have been able to see the departing squad. 'May Sol protect you,' he whispered.

Once the squad cleared the three-storey walls of the fort, the two GCRs levelled their hover flight to two feet then fell into single file to reduce wind drag and for easy movement through the various small farming structures that encircled Fort Grey. The GCRs were twenty feet long and half as wide so piloting around the streets with only a few feet on each side was tricky. There were two crew in each of the two GCRs, a pilot and a person manning the beam cannon turret mounted on the roof of the GCR about ten feet off the ground while in motion. Although these vehicles were large enough to allow up to six people to fit inside, Lieutenant Klon in the gunner seat of the lead GCR thought it would be best to conserve power in the repeller drive in case they needed to run. She did not know what from, but anything *was* possible. These vehicles were not too big but still required a lot of power to fly.

Three foot soldiers plodded along each side of the pair of GCRs, scanning for anything out of the ordinary. A trooper walked at each corner with the third in the middle with some nine feet between them. One soldier, the young private, found himself bringing up the rear of the formation behind the vehicles, which seemed safe enough for him. Another young soldier named Mark Pellar took point and was outfitted with extra sensor gear on his armour whilst the middle soldier on each side carried a beam weapon of a smaller variety than the vehicle mounted ones. It seemed command thought they might need the extra gear.

The group made good time as they had a slight tail wind spring up to push them along and the terrain was mostly flat leading away from the fort. They were moving through the fields travelling at an average speed of thirteen mph. After six hours of travelling open green fields and small clusters of trees, Mark caught sight of his first real landmark, the Brossan Hills.

Like many, he lived his whole life in the community around Fort Grey and had only heard stories of the Hills and the problems they had caused the farmers... now to see them was amazing. They were named after the laser technician who decided during the terraforming of Mars that this part of the Eden peninsula was too flat and added the hills against the wishes of the agriculture minister. When he died, they buried him in his precious hills. As a farm-boy, Mark could not help but smile as his armoured boots left barely noticeable prints in the lush green hills marring them for the time being at least.

The lead trooper to the left of the GCRs opened his respirator and let in the dense fragrant air. Although it was more difficult to breath, he inhaled deeply, almost as if needing the aromas of the open air. He could smell the grass in the fields and almost taste the small patches of white wild flowers growing on the leeward side of the hills.

'Close that respirator, trooper,' the pilot of the lead GCR snapped. He could see the trooper breaching protocol.

'Sir, these respirators filter everything. Sure, they make the air easier to breath, but it has no flavour!'

'I don't care, man. You're on active duty and the armour has to remain sealed.'

'Lighten up Tommy; you're a farm boy too. Don't you miss the smells of the land?'

'Yeah...'

'Cut the chatter you two and open your eyes for that wreckage! I don't want to be out here too long. And close that respirator, John!' Daniella said. She understood what the private was talking about. 'We can stop to smell the roses on the...'

'Heads up!' Mark cut in, 'I've got a signal on radar ... make that several contacts.'

'How many?' Daniella shouted.

'Lots, moving fast. Nearly forty mph! My God! They're...'

Static filled the air in the monitoring station for a long moment after that last message. Commander Martel was in the Comm. room monitoring the communications for the last hour. Now the channel was clear. No static. No voices. They were just gone, swallowed by something.

He hung his head in the silence he could not break and would never forget.

The tech behind him, though a veteran of many skirmishes, let a few tears escape for her lost friends and compatriots. She stood at rigid attention as she waited for her commander's orders.

Somehow the rest of the base knew as well. Not one sound echoed from the vehicle bay and the barracks both North and South were eerily silent. Not a soul moved. If not for the people standing or kneeling throughout the fortress, Fort Grey may well have looked abandoned.

After several minutes of this strained silence, Commander Martel emerged from the Communications building and announced the demise of the First Recon Squad, Fort Grey. The news hit like a thunderclap. Men and women cried and consoled one another. No one was unaffected, not even the usually stolid Paul Nivek, Blademaster of Second Recon, who bowed his head and did not move for what seemed an eternity, until the unit commanding officer, TJ Marso put his arm around him and lead him off to the barracks.

Commander Martel stood alone, stone-faced in the middle of the compound, staring at the star above him, Bane.

*****

CHAPTER III
Thursday, 18 March, 2251

The next day, began like most others, men and women that comprised a small part of Fort Grey's personnel stood on top of the south-facing walls. Their gleaming power armour emitted a faint hum as it resisted the dense atmosphere beginning to press against them. As always they had mounted the sloped walls to get the best view of Sol rising over the horizon. As it shone on them, they would quietly celebrate the rebirth of the light. There was no speech this day.

Below them in the southern quarter of the two thousand foot circle of houses and farming structures around the fort was a courtyard filled with the local residents. They concluded their welcoming ceremony for the sun as it peaked out through the crystals and haze in the southern sky.

This morning, however, one thing was different from the usual group of sun worshippers – there were now dozens of armoured men and women facing the star as it ascended into the sky, a number more than triple the usual amount. Most were praying for the safe return of Lieutenant Klon's recon squad though they knew for the most part that it was unlikely any of those unfortunate souls would be seen alive again. Training accidents were always serious with the nature of the weapons they carried and the weather systems beyond the walls.

Some of the people standing on the wall did not realize that more personnel, other than the First Recon, were missing from the Fort's ranks of roughly five-hundred troopers and support workers. Even the majority of the staff remaining within the walls did not yet know a second squad had already left the security of the fortress in the pre-dawn hours. It was the Second Recon Squad that had departed just after the setting of the rogue star, Bane under orders that kept the men and women of the Second Recon from talking to non-squad personnel.

*****

'Lieutenant Marso, Buzz come with me,' Commander Martel had said a few hours after he had made the announcement about the first recon. He took the two men down towards the narrow end of the medical bunker so as not to be overheard by persons who had no business knowing what was about to be said.

'TJ,' the Commander had started, 'we have no proof that the entire squad was wiped out, let alone anyone at all...'

'But sir,' TJ interrupted, 'it's been five hours since that last transmission. They were only six hours out. If they had gotten away from whatever is out there the patrol squad is only a few miles out and would have signalled us they had seen something of them by now. And frankly sir, we've seen and heard nothing since transmission terminated.'

'I know that much, but we still have no proof. I need to have proof, TJ, before I write them off and that's why you are going to take your people out tonight. You'll make for their last reported location. I want you to bring home the survivors or whatever you find out there.'

TJ had never seen the Commander this adamant before but he still had his point to make. 'If we go out there at night we'll be no better defended than they were. Hell, we don't even know what to defend against. I'm not thrilled about risking my people on this, sir.'

'TJ, I want to know what happened to my people,' he repeated.

'Sir, we heard what happened and it wasn't anything good,' Buzz said in a low voice.

'We heard nothing, young man. The transmission simply stopped.'

'Yes sir,' TJ said and waved at Buzz to end the discussion. He knew what the Commander meant; fear of the unknown was a terrible thing.

'Take three GCRs with you so you can make a secured camp once you get beyond the visual range of the fort.'

'We'll find them, sir.'

'Thanks... and TJ, this is on a need to know basis – I don't want to alarm anyone more than they are already.'

TJ nodded before turning and giving a quick glance at the young warrant officer.

'What?' Buzz said. He held out his arms as he too turned and followed TJ back into the heart of the base. 'It was a valid point.'

TJ sat against the hull of one of his three gophers, a slang term Buzz seemed to have started up. He was freshly rested and allowed himself a moment to sit back and watch as Sol rose up to shine on his squad. The black landscape slowly faded to the lush green of the fields and the green-grey haze that was the air. They had not made great time last night but they were now at a point beyond where most people from Fort Grey had ever been. He did not even want to guess what their average speed was. He did know, however, that they had travelled about sixty miles during the early night. That put them almost three-quarters of the way to where the First Recon should still be, or the debris at least.

There was one trooper in each of the three GCRs manning the beam cannon turrets throughout the night, which was a standard military practise. The GCRs were still hovering a foot off the ground and arranged in a triangle formation preventing easy access to the middle of the formation where the troopers not on shift could sleep, eat and rest. The makeshift fortress was in a slight dip in the field likely caused by a meteor strike thousands of years ago. In this location only the turrets and antennae were visible.

The field beyond the crater was covered in a lush, thick carpet of grass and the occasional flower patch. It was a beautiful area of the Eden peninsula, if only they could enjoy it as it was designed to be. There was not much cause for travel between the cities these days so they probably would not get the chance again, in fact no one in this squad had been much farther from Fort Grey than this point before.

Ashley Sanders rose in the middle of the GCRs and stretched as much as her armour allowed. She was of average height and build, which allowed her bountiful, chestnut brown hair to get all the attention. Her emerald green eyes did draw a few comments every now and then, as well. She still held the rank of Corporal despite her three years in the service of Fort Grey. She did not mind, however, the rigours of squad command just were not her game. Besides, she carried the same attitude as a Lieutenant, and used it to her advantage... and just for fun on occasion. To prove the point, she punted another trooper, Ken Michelson, in his boot with enough power-assisted force to slide him a foot or so into one of the GCR skids. The torn green grass and disturbed red dirt formed a small ridge as it piled up around him thanks to the slide.

'Bloody hell Ashley! You'll be bangin' up my armour if ya keep that up!' he snorted indignantly.

'Get up and shut up, you lazy oaf. We've got stuff to do today, and we can't have you lying around all day,' she teased playfully. 'Now use that fancy power armour of yours to lift your sorry behind out of that dent you put in the ground.'

'Who the hell made you Lieutenant, lady,' Ken barked and rose to his feet with clumps of dark red dirt clinging to his armour. Despite the harshness in his voice he managed to say it with a smile on his face.

'I decided to retire while you were sleeping, Ken,' TJ piped in.

Even the sombre Master Sergeant Paul Nivek, who was still melancholy after the news of the First Recon's demise, cracked an amused smile. He was almost as tall as TJ with a significantly larger build. He had shaved his head when it became obvious that it was going to leave on its own. Throughout the entire roster at Fort Grey, there was no one who could match him in skill with the blade.

Brenda Quinn-Dire was a rookie trooper of remarkable beauty to be in the military. Her helmet somehow covered her impossibly thick, dark brown hair but her sapphire eyes sparkled brightly. She had been listening to a lecture from the squad's heavy weapons specialist, Johnny Gentry, on various techniques for the class-3 beam cannon when the commotion broke out. She could not help herself and started to giggle madly and thus caused Johnny to smile patiently until he could continue with the lecture.

Master Sergeant Gentry was a large man, broad in the shoulder and usually quick to temper. His sandy blond hair was kept in a neat brush cut despite the itching it sometimes caused when he had his helmet on.

'A joke right?' panicked another of the squad's rookies, Chuck Gnaren. His height was a constant source of hazing while he was going through the academy. Many of the other cadets had referred to him in a most unaffectionate manner as *The Gnome*. His fuzzy little body certainly didn't help the situation any. The only thing allowing him to brush off the razzing was the fact he was not too bright. 'I mean there should be something like a vote before command of a squad is just handed over, right? She's not even next in line by rank.'

His comment only seemed to escalate the situation. Those that were smiling or laughing already began to laugh uncontrollably. The three gunners began to chuckle as well. Then after a snorting laugh from Austin Ferra, in the lead GCR, the concentration of the squad's other Blademaster, Dave Terry, was shot all to hell. The trooper with whom he was practising lost control. They lowered their blades and leaned against one another and laughed with the group.

'Look how happy you made everyone by stepping down, boss,' Buzz chimed in.

'What?' a stunned Chuck asked. 'I'm not happy, who'd be happy about that?'

'Oh no. Stop, stop!' pleaded Stephanie Williams in another GCR between gasps for breath.

TJ knew when facing a future of uncertainty every squad needed to laugh and relax but the mission still had to be done. 'All right everyone, how about we get this day over with? Paul, take point. Brenda, you're in front of me on the left side. Everyone else, you know where to go. Make sure you're all combat ready.'

'You're not really thinking we're going to have to fight are you, TJ?' Buzz voiced a concern likely felt by the others.

'Better to be safe,' he put a hand on Buzz's shoulder before ushering him into a vehicle.

'I guess just not looking forward to it is all.'

With a few giggles fading in the hustle of power armour coming to life again, they formed up and started off towards the Brossan Hills.

'Buzz, call in our progress and remember to use the codes in case we're dealing with pirates again,' TJ called back.

'Sure thing,' Buzz chirped back.

In the third GCR, Buzz punched the security codes into the scrambler and reported to the commander that in all reality, nothing had happened. Just before the signal terminated, there was a powerful squelch from the line. Buzz ripped the connection from the panel and gave his head a vigorous shake. After he had recovered, Buzz checked the other instruments to try to find a reason for the feedback and determined it was likely due to the weather system visible in the vicinity of the base. Once the connection was terminated he continued his surveillance.

The next two hours passed painfully slow but was uneventful. The formation passed seemingly undisturbed clusters of trees, unmarked acres of grasslands all leading up to the last reported location of the First Recon, but there was no sign of them. The hope of finding their compatriots diminished greatly for the first time.

Buzz triple checked all his readouts for a sign of anything man-made other than this group of wandering troops but to no avail. The weather tracking system had the longest range within this atmosphere but even it could not read any anomalies apart from the storm seventy miles back towards Fort Grey. While visual scanning range was limited to half a mile and ground radar could give an idea of movement at up to five miles the weather tracker was good to a hundred miles. All together these systems provided a good picture of the area if you read them properly but there was nothing to see.

*****

CHAPTER IV
Thursday, 18 March, 2251

The Second Recon squad out of Fort Grey was about to clear the gently rolling hills towards Fort Saturn, when the first signs of conflict became apparent. On the north side of the hills ahead, a twenty-foot long horizontal gouge dug deep through the brown topsoil, exposing the red Martian rock beneath. A beam cannon shot was the obvious culprit judging by the burning of the surrounding grass down to the roots.

'TJ!' Paul called out. They insisted during situations calling for combat protocol, he be referred to as *Kain*. It was a call sign he had picked out for himself and everyone let him have his way.

'Yeah?' TJ replied, looking up towards his point man.

'Looks like there's been some action around here.'

'Okay Kain, use the thermal imaging to see how long ago this was and if there's anything hiding out there. Iceman, you and Brenda... I mean QD... keep those cannons ready. Dave, you give close-in coverage for them.'

'Yes, sir,' Dave or as he preferred in situations like these, *Duke*, squeezed in the middle of the orders.

'...Ashley, Ken, Steph, and Marshal, you're with me,' TJ finished before plodding off towards the giant scratch.

Just before they stepped out of the GCRs, the pilots swung their sleds back into the protective triangular formation. This time the sleds were on level ground and rather than providing a simple rest stop provided cover for Kain while he scanned the area. TJ and the four troopers walked off towards the scorch mark and left the triangle of GCRs well behind them along with the additional armoured personnel. They were too vulnerable without the sleds to provide cover for TJ's liking but protocol said there had to be a safe base of operation while they went ahead to conduct the search. As they investigated the area, it was almost immediately obvious a beam cannon from a GCR or a similar vehicle rather than a personal use cannon, had dug this trench. Looking around they saw that debris lined the small valley between the two hills to either side. There were pieces ranging in size from a busted rivet to two full size armour plates.

The two plates of armour drew the attention of the investigators because of their apparent lack of damage. Primary evidence concluded the two panels were actually one panel that had been cleaved in two, with the severed edges melted to boot. The scariest part was that this panel had come from a GCR, and was otherwise undamaged.

'Looks like the shooter was on that hill, firing down,' Ashley said waving her arm in a sweeping motion from the north hill to the gash.

'If it had to fire with this much determination,' Ken said, indicating the length and depth of the mark, 'and by the presence of this panel I'd have to say they could not have made it out of whatever situation they found themselves in.'

'This would mean that they cashed in. They ain't on this side of the hill, which means we have to go over the top,' Marshal concluded, pointing at the hill.

'Let's go have a look then? And stay sharp! Whatever destroyed the GCR could easily still be around here,' TJ said.

Cautiously, the group scaled the slope of the hill, weapons at the ready, although not activated. They crawled to keep a low profile up the last forty feet of the hill and peered over the tiny summit. There, in an artificially enhanced valley, sat almost one and a half transports looking like a type of the large transport hovercraft, BR-AT-217. The part of the broken transport that was no longer present housed the reactor. At least the question of how half of a massive armoured vehicle could go missing was answered. The debris field, however, was too large for only one section, which meant another vehicle had also met its end here.

'Do you think it was one of ours?' Ashley said, indicating the blast hole.

Since the men in the group got to use call signs, she decided she would have one as well. She had chosen to use *Viper*. It was often commented, quietly of course, that it suited her.

'I don't think so. It was more likely the convoy escort. Most likely it was stationed out of Fort Saturn,' TJ concluded.

'Yep, you're right, chief. I can make out a *FS* emblem on one of the larger pieces.' Ken indicated a section of hull plating partially buried in the red and green blended valley.

Unlike the others of the squad, Ken preferred to be called Ken. However, a childhood nickname seemed to have stuck and become his call sign, *Dolly*, for reasons he was not about to share.

'Yeah! I see it, Dolly,' TJ grinned. Ken glowered, 'That first BRAT looks like it's still in good shape. Okay, Marshal, you and Viper check out that one and you other two come with me to look through the wreckage and see if we can see what did this.'

They picked themselves up and jogged down the far side of the hill, beyond the sight of the Recon Squad's triangle. About halfway down, Marshal and Viper broke off to the right towards the intact BRAT. The others, meanwhile, made a direct line for the field of wreckage centred on the deepest and newest part of the valley.

Around the valley and crater the carpet of torn grass, red rock and debris stretched from the rear of the intact BRAT for about two or three hundred yards. The scrap consisted of bits of various sizes and varying states of burial. The smell of burnt wiring still hung heavy in the valley.

When they reached the wreckage TJ walked around, looking at all the parts and scraps lying about in disarray. He picked up pieces here or there but he always looked to the sky. He had the notion stuck in his mind that whatever had taken out the First Recon had come from up there. Try as he might, it was a feeling he could not shake. Maybe it was something in the surprise of the last transmission from the squad.

TJ glanced up the opposite wall of the valley for signs of a land attack, hoping his fears were unfounded, but found evidence telling a different story. The grass and shrubs on the slope were cracked and crushed down flat in three separate trails. From the width of the first two trails, nearest the remaining vehicle, the two BRATs slid into the valley instead of hovering indicating a possible loss of power. The accompanying GCR, however, rolled in, judging by the appearance of heavy dents in the turf along the trail.

During one of his sky-watching episodes, TJ thought he caught a glimpse of something moving out of the corner of his eye. Before he could look, Dolly ambled up to him at a leisurely pace. Ken was a big man with the power of a bear but always calm – unless someone called him Dolly – then he seemed to puff up like he hoped the name would bounce off of him that time or maybe the next.

'Hey chief, what are you staring at?'

'What? Mmm... nothing, I guess. What did you and Steph find?'

'Looks like pirates did this one in. Something about it just doesn't fit though. Don't know what it is.'

'I think I've solved that puzzle for you,' TJ stated as he reconstructed in his mind what he thought might have happened. 'It seems that this convoy was already done for, including the GCR, but both of the BRATs were still intact for the most part. Due to the damage, however, they weren't going anywhere. Then maybe your pirates came along for some easy pickings and accidentally nuked one of their prize catches. I think that our Recon folk were running from something and came by this way. Then a stray shot, either from them or the chasers, went through the armour and hit the reactor.'

'That'd explain why some of the carbon scorch marks are older than the others. Oh, and by the way, keeping those two possibilities in mind, either the pirates took the cargo of conductors or somebody's shot vaporized it when the reactor went.'

'Let's hope for the latter. Steph!' he yelled even though his external speakers could have easily done the job, 'meet us over by Marshal and Viper.'

Over near the damaged BRAT, Stephanie waved and began to move off towards the whole BRAT.

'Dolly, tell the triangle that we've found the convoy. We've got one more transport to check. Then we'll be on our way back,' TJ said

'Roger that,' Dolly replied, obviously happy to be leaving this destruction. As he began his transmission, they both heard the sound of beam cannons ripping the air and the faint clashing of blade on blade.

'Ssssss...an't talk...sssss... ittle busy he...ssssss...'

'That sounded like Buzz. Come on, we have to get the others. Call him back and see if they need help,' TJ ordered.

As TJ and Dolly ran back to meet the others at the second BRAT, Dolly transmitted back to Buzz. He nearly stumbled when an animal-like screech blasted through his headphones before the computer buffers could compensate for the increased volume. By the time he had recovered, TJ and Stephanie were standing beside him. Dolly thought he could still hear the screech, though it now seemed to be quieter than before. Even after his hearing had returned to normal the faint screech remained.

'Do you guys hear that?' he asked quietly.

'Ummm, yeah. Yeah I do! It's getting louder,' Stephanie said.

Almost on cue, five mythological creatures emerged on the top of the hill. They almost looked comical until you got a good look into their faces, then the impression died fast. There were dark coloured horns protruding from above their pointed ears, and equally blackened pincers on the sides of the creature's wickedly fanged mouth. But the most disturbing of all their features, was the vicious glow from their eyes... eyes that seemed fake until you noticed there was no blinking or movement. TJ knew they were being watched.

They were graceful creatures despite being about the size of an Old Earth grizzly bear. Their deep rust coloured skin had little or no fur with the appearance of worn leather under which there was hard, sculpted muscles and powerful hind legs. Their fore limbs looked well-muscled and almost as large but with a bone-like protrusion from each forearm, like scythes extending backward from below the wrist joint. They also had a large triangular fan extending from each of its shoulders, ending in three dark-green foot-and-a-half long fingers. Sitting up there in a crouch and not moving allowed their dark colour to blend them into the ridge line.

The three humans froze where they stood at the sight of these oddities. None of them knew exactly what to do as the things were easily the same size as they were in their armour! The creatures seemed uncertain of what to do and sat there. Maybe the current backdrop of the field debris was probably confusing the creatures, TJ figured. If that was the case, it was only a matter of time before they saw them.

Marshal, who had been inside the intact BRAT with Viper until now, chose this moment to come flying out of the side entrance-way. He was clearly excited about something, judging by the frantic waving of his arms.

'Hey, Lieutenant! We've found the... Oh shit!' He dove back into the doorway.

The *fingers* on the back of these gargoyle-like creatures rose in an instant. Brilliant green spans of light appeared between the fingers forming large wings, and with a screech and a powerful downward stroke the wings of light lifted the creatures into the air.

They swooped down on the threesome standing in the valley, obviously now able to differentiate what these humans looked like from the useless scrap in the field. During their dive, their wings moved up and down rhythmically to maintain the desired height or rate of descent. The green spans of light pulsed with the flapping motion of the wings, on for down and off for up.

The creatures let out a ferocious howl with more than a hint of the glee of a predator on the hunt. That sound was enough to break the temporary paralysis holding TJ and Dolly. Ken bolted first, followed closely by TJ who had to pass Stephanie to get to cover and noticed she was not moving. He grabbed the loading handle on her pack and half dragged her away.

When he saw the monsters closing the gap rapidly, TJ realized that pulling her the entire way was not an option. He shoved the stunned trooper behind him and brought his blade to life to protect her until she regained her senses. The leading edge of the bony projections from their forearms lit up in an unnatural glow when the diving creatures were no more than sixty feet away, similar to the magnetically contained beams from a beam cannon.

'Ten blades to one. That figures,' TJ muttered as he set himself for the oncoming battle. 'Hey! I'm going to need some help out here. I'm not a Blademaster, you know!' he bellowed, not daring to look away. 'Snap out of it Steph, I need you here.'

With no time to wait for a response, TJ swung his blade to meet the lead gargoyle's scythes. Freed energy erupted from where the two energy fields met and the little crystal shards chewed at the creature's plasma. He could not remember ever encountering anything that could stop a blade aside from a magnetic field. Wondering about how this thing could produce a magnetic field that strong would have to wait for now. TJ countered the one-two slicing of the creature's attack but missed the second gargoyle's move against him. This thing looked like a prize fighter in its swings though no punches were landed – instead the damage came from the blazing scythes on the outside of the arm.

An impact from a swing he failed to block, rocked his armour but left him standing. He looked at the armour status readout on his heads-up-display and realized it was not serious, he was lucky. The glancing blow had sheared off the neck protection plate on his right shoulder, only metal thankfully. It was fortunate TJ had stopped the first gargoyle where he did because the creature now obstructed the only clear route to him. The others had to find an alternate route, which gave him time, not much but it was something.

The creatures adapted quickly to this change in plan and struck at TJ before he had completely regained his balance. His predicament became far worse with the third attack from a swooping gargoyle. As it had corrected for its leader's abrupt stop, it grabbed at TJ's head. Fortunately, the armour's almost aerodynamic design prevented the creature from getting any sort of grip. The grip was enough that he was knocked backwards instead of being ripped apart at the neck. The force of the blow sent him tumbling into Stephanie, which sent her flying back as well.

Two of the five creatures attacking him still lurked on the ground within striking distance, while the third continued to flutter overhead. TJ could not even begin to fathom where the other two were hiding. He jumped to his feet almost immediately and got ready for the next hit.

'Shit!' TJ thought, 'I don't even know what's going to kill me.'

The gargoyle-thing he had encountered first made a move to strike but was stopped short by an unexpected stumble. It glanced down at the emerald green fountain of glowing shards poking out from its massive chest, and then fell without looking up again. The other creature started to step back when TJ's blade swung through its midsection, cutting it neatly in two. The nature of the blade cauterized the slash, mercifully limiting the amount of blood but a green ooze began to spread slowly from the separated body parts.

TJ looked away from the fallen mound of flesh beside him to see Viper standing over the dead creature she had punctured from behind. Behind her, Dolly and Marshal were in a heated battle against one of the gargoyles. TJ and Viper turned to assist when the creature that had been circling above dived into the fray. With its slash it creased Marshal's backpack with one of its forearm blades. The hit did not injure Marshal at all but it destroyed his power cell, rendering him practically immobile since the armour was too heavy to move with any kind of speed.

The gargoyle Dolly was now fighting alone saw Marshal's actions slow significantly and went in for the kill. It lifted one of its wings and lit the brilliant green field between the fingers, which deflected Dolly's swing the same way a blade would and knocked him back. The creature then brought its right scythe across and down Marshal's torso, slashing into him from the left shoulder to the right hip. To finish the job it then cut off his head cleanly with a slash from its left arm. The remainder of Marshal went limp and fell to the ground, adding a more red to the Martian landscape.

The gargoyle creature howled with glee over the fallen human and lifted its arms in victory, which ended when Dolly buried his blade into its side. That particular howl was silenced forever, while others, a little way off, continued to carry on the wind.

The other gargoyle that had sliced Marshal's power cell jumped into the air and flew off in a north-easterly direction. The last creature that had come in with the group suddenly appeared to the left of their field of vision and flew to join its compatriot. TJ snapped his head around in the direction it had come from to see the lifeless form of Stephanie, her armour torn apart in the middle.

'Damn!' TJ sighed.

'Oh Steph, no!' Viper cried, letting her usual cool slip as she ran over to her fallen friend.

Dolly stood over Marshal's body hanging his head. Blade still buzzing, TJ walked over to his big friend and pulled him away from the sight.

'You did all that you could do, Ken. No one could have saved him.'

'I know, but that doesn't make it any easier to swallow.'

'Come on, we can't stay here any longer. We have to get back to the triangle and find out what's left of our rides home and the people watching them,' TJ said as he picked up Marshal's blade.

Viper walked up to the two men and glanced only briefly at the trooper's remains. She was holding Stephanie's blade in her hand. Her smooth, steady voice had returned, 'It wasn't even fired up once. Looks like these monsters were hungry too, there's hardly anything left of her,' she turned away from the body at her feet. 'By the way Lieutenant, Marshal was about to say that we found what is left of the First Recon. They're inside the BRAT.'

'They're still alive?' Dolly asked.

'Could be, we didn't get a chance to look.'

'Okay, let's move these two bodies into that BRAT and we'll have a look at the First Recon,' TJ announced.

As he moved off towards the BRAT, Dolly began to move Marshal into the shelter and Viper dragged the near-empty armour, which was once Stephanie, to meet up with them. Inside the dark cargo bay of the BRAT, TJ found a GCR buried amongst the cargo, still hovering. Against the far wall he saw six suits of rough looking battle armour as well. All of them were switched *on* according to the imaging readout on his HUD, although he still had no idea of which of the occupants were still alive.

'Hey now! Who's in here?' he barked.

'Two of us sir. Maybe three but I haven't checked lately. We ran out of medical supplies a long time ago. I know for sure that it's me and Martin beside me. The Lieutenant was still alive in the gopher but she's been quiet for a while now,' the armoured trooper on the far left said.

TJ recognized the suit as belonging to the private Daniella had been training before the First Recon had left Fort Grey. TJ moved past the two troopers before they could get to their feet and went around to the far side of the GCR. What he saw there was incredible. The side of the GCR looked like a meteor had hit it. Long slashes decorated the heavily impacted rear hatchway, nothing seemed to have gotten through to the interior however. Using the two blades he had, TJ carefully and patiently cut back the hatch to gain access to the inside.

'Why didn't you guys open this earlier?' TJ asked harshly.

In response, the young private, Erik Krushell, lifted his blade hilt and hit the *activate* switch. Nothing happened.

'Ah, sorry,' he realized without a working blade there was no way that the two of them could have opened the GCR armour

TJ peeled back the plating he had softened with the blades and looked inside. He saw armoured form of Daniella slumped over the ruined gunner controls. He scrambled into the crippled GCR and plugged into her bio-readout jack. Her vital signs were low but stable, thanks to the suit.

He stepped out of the GCR to see the two troopers helping to bring in the bodies of Marshal and Stephanie. TJ made his way to the control section of the BRAT and slid into the pilot's chair. He took a moment to absorb the events of the last ten minutes before he did anything else.

'Readouts look good for this thing. Power is a bit low and the radar is gone but she'll fly,' he said as he turned on the repeller drives, 'Hang on back there. We're going to take this crate with us.'

Scraps of blasted armour fell from the BRAT, some belonging to it and other bits not, as it lifted itself up to the standard cruising height of three feet. As it moved off towards the hill Dolly came to the control cabin.

'TJ, this isn't a military transport.'

'What are you talking about? It was sitting right in front of the other BRAT, and it was military,' TJ said, more than a little puzzled.

'There is no sign of any weapon crates. Just a couple of scrap crystals.'

'Boy, this day is just full of surprises, isn't it?'

The BRAT cleared the hill and drifted into full view of the triangle of GCRs. It floated towards the formation with a slight shudder as it crossed the last six hundred feet and came to an ungraceful stop beside the makeshift fortress. All around the triangle were tracks of vaporized grass and dirt and about ten motionless gargoyles in various stages of dismemberment.

TJ stepped out of the side hatch of the BRAT with Viper at his side and down onto a patch of burnt grass. When they saw their commanding officer, a head emerged from each of the two closest GCRs. Several badly dented suits of armour emerged from the interior of the grouping. They looked weary even in the rigid armour. He had never seen battle armour look saggy before.

'Lieutenant, good to see ya!' Chuck yelled, 'Where are the others?'

'Steph and Marshal didn't make it. Dolly and a couple of First Reconers are looking after Lieutenant Klon. How'd we do here?'

'They bounced us pretty good. They got QD and banged Duke up really good. Austin got smoked in GCR Three over there,' replied Buzz.

'Damn,' TJ snorted, 'Salvage what you can out of that GCR, including Austin. Then I want Iceman to detonate it. Everyone load up! We're goin' home!'

'Hey TJ,' Kain called, 'got some news for you.'

'Yeah, what is it?'

'I was scanning like you told me to and I was getting nothing. That is, until Buzz called in our progress as per our schedule. Then those things seemed to pop out of nowhere, like the transmission let them find us.'

'Are you saying it was my fault?' Buzz asked.

'Hell no, I'm saying what happened,' Kain tried to sooth him.

'Sounds like they were waiting for us,' Iceman added, 'Why else would they have stuck around?'

'You make it sound like they're intelligent, Johnny,' Kain said.

'Think about it. They fly, right? This we know. And ninety percent or so of all flying creatures that I know about live in trees, or at least in elevated areas. And frankly boys, these hills aren't that tall. So they wouldn't have stayed around here for so long unless they knew that more prey was coming.'

'You think those things are from this planet?!' Buzz was

shocked.

'How should I know? This planet has mutated so many of the animals that we brought over it could have started out as anything.'

'Yeah, like what?'

'I don't know man, all I know is they were waiting,' Iceman kicked the dirt in frustration.

'And,' Viper put in, 'they were here to kill. Not for food, despite what happened to Steph, but more like a war. Animals don't work that way, usually.'

'You're right. We're leaving now! Grab a couple of those things and toss them into the cargo bay, then get in yourselves. Ashley, I want you to take the second GCR, Ken you get the BRAT,' TJ ordered as he made his way to the lead GCR.

The smaller vehicles powered up and escorted the huge BRAT out of the combat zone. Once clear and on route to Fort Grey with long grass kissing the bottom of the vehicles, they slid into flanking positions around the transport. There was a slight head wind rustling the grass beneath them and bending the sparse trees. They sky had a deeper grey, almost blue colouring since Sol had set and Bane now ruled the sky. Their departure from the hills was punctuated by a blast vaporizing the scrapped GCR and the gargoyles lying around it.

'Did you happen to use enough detonators Johnny?' TJ asked light-heartedly.

'I had a couple of extras lying around,' he quipped back.

They surged forward, making the best possible time for Fort Grey. Even though they were pushing the old BRAT as fast as it could go, they only managed about twenty miles-per-hour. It was well after dark by the time they came to rest in front of the fortress walls. They signalled the Watch to get them to open the huge armoured doors. Rumbling doors announced to the base the arrival of the troops and the Fort welcomed home the men and women of the First and Second Recon Squads, Fort Grey Division.

Despite nearly two hundred people flanking the convoy, there was a profound silence. TJ had called ahead a report on what they had found out there, about an hour before they arrived. He thought he heard a faint screech as he terminated the transmission but it did not matter, they were inside the fortress now. Medical teams scurried to the wounded and techs came to assess the damage to vehicles and armour.

An Honour guard appeared shortly after the convoy stopped to remove the fallen.

The silence remained for the rest of the night as the squad members were debriefed and the bodies appropriately laid to rest. The gargoyles-creatures' bodies were taken to the medical bunker to await examination in the morning.

Tonight was for tears, goodbyes and remembrances.

*****

CHAPTER V
Friday, 1 April, 2251

Commander Martel sat at his desk with his head in his hands.

It was first dawn on April first, although lately it did not seem to matter what the date was, the bad news never seemed to go away. The last two mornings at Fort Grey had brought with them the news of at least twenty deaths. Nine of those were his own people, and now on this morning he was down another four more good people.

'Well, at least the number was getting smaller,' Martel said softly to himself.

He would have felt worse if the top brass had known the stats. Lately, however, he was unable to contact any of his superiors. All long range signals seemed blocked. Even communication with the District Command in Fort Saturn was disrupted. At least he did not have to deal with that aspect of his day.

'There's always a bright side, or at least, somewhat a less dark side.'

'Sir?' TJ asked. He had been sitting in the office for the past fifteen minutes.

'Oh, sorry TJ; I was just thinking out loud,' Martel said.

'Sir, as I was saying, I had a technician check out the recording systems on the BRAT we brought back and I think we might have a bigger problem than some missing weapon materials.'

'Wonderful. Let's hear it.'

TJ stood up and made his way across the woven blue carpet to the audio system of the office. He began to enter the selection of the record he wanted and the security codes that would give him access to the black-box recordings from the BRAT. Once the track was available to him, he picked up the remote control and returned to his seat.

'Now, these are a group of recordings taken from the entire history of the BRAT. It appears to have been a civilian transport so most of it is gibberish. You know, things like *how's the wife*, and so on. But the clips I've chosen seem to be the most relevant.'

< Male voice > *Miles Research Station, this is BRAT 14831 – departing from construction bay 916 for duty at your facility.*
< Male voice > *Confirmed 14831, we await your arrival.*
< Pause >
< Female voice > *M.R.S. Control, this is BRAT 14831 on route to New Venus for crystal shipment.*
< Male voice > *Roger 14831. Last run for that old crate, eh?*
< Female voice > *Yep! I'll miss her.*
< Pause >

TJ stopped the recording, 'I put those clips in to show the uneventful history of this vehicle. This next part was dated March 13.'

< Female voice > *M.R.S. Control, do you copy?*
< Male voice, distant > *Where the hell are they?*
< Female voice > *Increase the imaging on the scope – what are those things?*
< Male voice > *Shit! They're moving this way. Get us outa here!*
< Female voice > *Hold on, we're breaking for Fort Saturn.*
< Pause >

'The next clip was the night of the March 16,' said TJ.

< Female voice > *Military convoy, this is BRAT 14831. We are under attack by ... Ahh! Look out! Bobby! (Sounds of screeching)*
< Male voice > *BRAT 14831, what is your location. BRAT 14831, what is – I think I see it. What are those? Oh Shit! ...*

'It cuts out after that,' TJ finished.
Silence hung over the office, a heavy silence. It pressed down on TJ more than anything he had ever felt before. TJ knew enough to keep quiet until the Commander spoke. He knew how the Commander dealt with the death of anyone whether they were under his command or not. Hearing it now, first-hand like this, the commander must be in torment. He knew also what the Commander was going to say next. It was obvious.
'That would indicate,' Martel started slowly, '...your BRAT wasn't part of the military convoy. You said you only found the

two BRATs, correct?' TJ nodded. 'So where's the other military BRAT? This isn't good, Lieutenant Marso. Those transport BRATs could have defended themselves against an entire squad of Blademasters. Whatever these things are, they're a major threat. We can't let this one go.'

'Yes, sir,' TJ said, as he stood.

Commander Martel leaned over his desk and snapped on the intercom, 'Get Major Harte in here and patch me through to communications.'

TJ had been expecting the order to move his troops out to deal with the problem at hand. Instead, he was left hanging while the Commander went about his own tasks. It was unusual for a detachment not to be sent out immediately in a verified threat situation. The fact that this did not fall into usual protocol left TJ perplexed. There was a short pause before TJ said, 'Sir, I don't...'

Before he could finish his objection to the Commander's course of action, the door opened Amanda Harte. She was out of breath and slightly dishevelled, and obviously freshly awakened. When she saw TJ in attendance she tried, with limited success to improve her appearance. After a few moments of fussing it became apparent her efforts were futile. She stopped and glared at TJ as if her condition was his fault. Lieutenant TJ quickly turned away to address his original concern.

'Sir, I...' He made even less headway this time.

'Major Harte, I'm impressed to see you here so quickly. It wasn't a matter that was so urgent as to arrive in this manner.'

Martel indicated the half-buttoned shirt, which barely concealed her belly button, clearly not conforming to military dress standards. 'Sorry, sir.' She continued to finish dressing, all the while firing searing glances at TJ, who pointedly looked away.

'What we have here is a very dangerous situation, Major,' he continued when she had straightened herself out, 'it seems...'

'Commander, this is Communications,' a young female voice crackled over the intercom.

'One moment,' he said to TJ and Amanda, 'Yes, Comm; get me Fort Saturn.'

'Yes, sir. I'll try again,' there was a slight pause, accompanied by the click-clack of hurriedly typed keys, 'Sir, I am unable to reach Fort Saturn. Like before, the channel is jammed.' Another pause. 'All the channels are jammed. All I get is static. It's like the signals are being eaten up by something.'

'Keep trying, Sergeant.'

'Yes, sir,' she said, a hint of frustration in her voice.

'Sir, if I may,' TJ interrupted, 'we encountered the same type of interference in the field. It occurred right before the creatures attacked us. The records of the First Recon show the same.'

'I gather then that you feel this fortress will fall under attack?'

'If he's right, sir, then I should get the facility's defences up and running,' snapped Amanda professionally. She turned and started for the door.

'Just a minute, Amanda,' he shook his head and muttered to himself. 'Why is everyone in such a hurry to leave my office this morning?'

Amanda was caught as far off guard as TJ had been and stopped in mid-stride. TJ allowed himself a tiny smirk at her expense.

'You'll do no such thing, the base is perfectly secure. Neither of the squads reported seeing these creatures anywhere near this part of the peninsula. More likely they will make a play for Fort Saturn and that's why I need you to take two squads to Fort Saturn immediately. You must warn them of the threat we've uncovered. TJ, your squad will be one of the escorts. You've had experience with at least some of what we're dealing with. If Lieutenant Klon is up to it, have her new squad provide support for your people and pull double duty to protect you, Major. I know this will be awkward for both of you but we'll get a better response time if the message comes from a higher-ranking officer.'

'Then, using your logic, you should come, sir,' TJ said.

'I would but I have to stay here unfortunately,' he held out a communiqué from the pile on his desk, 'It came in from Port Mars before we lost contact. For some idiotic reason, they want all commanders to stay at their posts until further notice. Something about Council inspections, a tour or some other nonsense. With this transmission interference I may very well be here the rest of my life.'

'But you most likely will be attacked here sir.'

'You don't know that, Major. Besides, I'm safer here than out there and you know I'd rather go than stay, but that message to Fort Saturn has to go today. I have my orders and now, you have yours. Both squads are to be ready for a morning departure.' He turned away from them and stared out his window overlooking the south barracks and, in the distance, the training compound.

TJ and Amanda stared at the Commander's back for a moment before heading out of his office. As they came down the last flight of stairs, Amanda spun on TJ and stopped him cold.

'I don't know what you did in there to get me assigned to a field duty but you'd better believe that when I give you an order out there, you're going to jump! You got that *Lieutenant* Marso?'

TJ was shocked at this outburst, unexpected as it was, he did not immediately know what to do or say except, 'Yes, Ma'am,' and salute in proper military fashion.

'Don't get smart,' she snapped a half-hearted salute in return and stormed off to get ready herself.

Buzz was standing outside the door during this scene, unseen by either of the two officers. He cautiously watched the Major march off towards her barracks. Only when he knew that she was out of range did he walk up to the still stunned TJ.

'She's got a great ass, eh chief?' Buzz smiled, trying to get a reaction.

'Um, what? Oh Buzz. Right, yeah,' stammered TJ, 'Look, the squad goes out tomorrow morning again. Diplomatic mission, I think – either that or pony express. I want two GCRs readied as well.'

'Already started, sir. I figured we might be going out pretty quick here.'

'Great; good Job, Buzz.'

'I'm not done yet, TJ,' Buzz said with mocked indignation.

'So sorry, sir. Pleeeeasse forgive your humble servant, master,' TJ bowed low.

'Thank you, as you were,' Buzz smiled. 'As I was about to say, those two privates we picked up at the convoy site have been assigned to us. Also, we have two replacements, a Private Peter Davies and Private Marsha Brown. Both have some crowd-control experience.'

There was a pause; TJ eyed Buzz carefully. 'Yeah, I'm done,' Buzz laughed.

'Whew! That's good. Get them ready and fill them in on everything. We froze once, I don't want that to happen again, it costs too much.'

'I've got the senior troopers drilling that point home right now.'

They walked in silence to the middle of the compound and began to gather the squad around to begin the preparations. At the far east-end of the training area, Daniella could be seen beginning to muster her squad. The Fort was abuzz again and the anticipation for the upcoming day could be felt everywhere.

*****

CHAPTER VI
Saturday, 2 April, 2251

The morning had a relaxed look about it. Men and women strolled about the Fort Grey base area as if nothing much was wrong. The image would have been that of tourist-poster quality except for the simple yet plainly obvious fact that there were two full combat-ready platoons assembling in the middle. Almost every trooper was eager, most notably the newer troopers, if not flat out excited to head out and meet fearsome creatures everyone now referred to as Gargoyles. While it appeared relaxed, the atmosphere inside the fortress was hectic beneath the surface. Daniella entered the vehicles bay at the east end of Fort Grey and stopped with a smile at her old friend, Amanda Harte barking orders left and right. Wherever Major Harte's gaze wandered, people jumped even if they were already doing something. Obviously, she had been at them for a while.

'Good to see nothing has changed while I was out of it,' said Daniella, her smile widening.

'What do you...' Amanda rounded on the speaker before she turned to see Daniella still smiling. 'Hi there! Well, don't you look good? You had me scared for a while after TJ brought you in.'

'That reminds me of why I came. Have you seen TJ today?'

'What do you want with that dodo?' Amanda sneered.

'I want to thank him, for one thing. And for another, I would like to go over our mission details,' Daniella said seriously.

'Well,' Amanda continued to snarl, 'He's at the end of the bay, helping his squaddies put the finishing touches on their GCRs.'

'Thanks, Amanda,' she said as she started down the bay, 'I still don't like him either, you know,' she called back over her shoulder. Behind her, she could hear her friend starting out again with her orders. Occasionally a flurry of footsteps would announce one group or another trying desperately to get out of her way.

Daniella had to pass several GCRs to get to the back end of the hanger. There were GCRs that were inactive, being readied, under repairs from the last excursion and a couple of new ones being built. The staff at Fort Grey was renowned for their efficiency at utilizing available resources to construct some of the best equipment on the Eden peninsula.

She went to the last stall in the vehicle bay before she found TJ. He was working with a tech crew on the rebuilding of a GCR to replace the one he had lost on his search and rescue mission. Huge yellow robotic arms twisted and bent in a blur of motion. Low-strength beams welded and textured frame sections, while high-powered lasers cut the necessary parts from a sheet of silvery meta-steel being generated by an industrial production fabrication machine.

The tech crew stood at various points along the construction, two techs beside the IP, monitoring speed and scanning the meta-steel for flaws in the strength of the processed material. One tech was next to the fabricator and the other next to him, both watching the readouts for possible problems. Another tech was above the construction frame monitoring the assembly. Off to the side of the project, the last of the six-man team was going over specs with TJ. That was where Daniella headed, steering well clear of the swirl of mechanical arms.

'And the wing needs to be a bit more like this,' TJ gestured with his hands to indicate the angle.

'Right,' started the tech, 'so that way there is less lift when the wind...' The tech made a cross-sweep with his hand across the diagram. 'No problem.'

'Great! And the rest?'

'Again, no problem, TJ.'

'Thanks,' TJ replied. The tech walked over to his team, bobbing his head up and down, 'Daniella! Hey, how are you?'

'Very well TJ, umm... thanks to you, of course,' she smiled shyly. She was not used to saying exactly what was on her mind.

'Hey, listen I know how you're feeling. You don't have to say anything, Daniella. Honestly, I wasn't expecting to find you alive,' he smiled.

'I know. I know the frame of mind you had to be in on your way out there, but I still had to say it, TJ. Thanks for coming out there for me,' she was blushing now.

He could sense she was more than a little uncomfortable with where this conversation may be headed so he tried to end this topic before something was said that could not be taken back. 'You're very welcome Daniella. You know I'd do it again.'

She smiled with tears in her eyes. She leaned in close to him and gave him a quick kiss on the lips. When she backed up a bit, her smile was still there and her hand went to her lips briefly.

His eyes were wide with surprise, but while he was still surprised her shyness got the better of her and she looked away. Her gaze fell on the group of techs looking at her with various expressions. Now she was embarrassed and totally forgot about going over mission details. TJ began to speak but she was gone before anything came out.

TJ failed to notice the lead tech walk up beside him. He wore a thinly disguised look of amusement behind his full-face safety shield but managed to speak clearly.

'Sir, a couple of questions if I may.'

'Hmm? Yeah,' he looked down the bay after Daniella for a moment, 'yeah, sure. How can I help?' He turned back to the task at hand.

*****

The two squads planned to travel in the best light of each day they had to be out there, in order to lessen the chance of an ambush. They had no idea if these things were nocturnal or even if they were out there but it was the safest option. This would also allow them the best opportunity to dig themselves in each night and keep the troops relaxed. With a detailed travel plan laid out, the two squads left Fort Grey in the height of the morning, after D200 hours. The caravan was large and well-armed but it had all the urgency of a walk through the park.

They even kept their formation more like a group of friends out for a stroll rather than a strict military procession. Armoured troopers sauntered along beside the slow-moving GCRs in groups of twos and threes. Making their way through the satellite small buildings they walked around the structures rather than sticking to a determined path, the casualness giving the local population no cause for worry. Once they were clear of the heavily armoured walls of the fort, chatter was restricted; however to local band frequencies only.

Unlike the troops, the GCRs held themselves in the standard, combat military convoy order. The carefully arranged zigzag pattern allowed all five vehicles to fire forward. The old BRAT had been repaired and recommissioned for this mission.

The group progressed at a steady pace for two hours, travelling a total of eleven miles. Their formation, if it could be called such never really broke at any point of the trip. Many of the twenty-five people travelling had been expecting some kind of action by now so were extremely bored leading to the occasional discharge of a beam cannon quickly followed by a profuse bout of apologies and much laughter. A couple of troopers would snap their blades to life and perform a non-aggressive sabre dance with flashes from the blades highlighting their armour until they realized the convoy was not going to wait for them and had to run to catch up.

TJ sauntered to the right of the convoy and talked with his Blademaster, Paul Nivek. 'I'm confused, ya know. I mean, what's her angle? I know she feels the same as Amanda when it comes to me, but that kiss wasn't just a thank you kiss. I can tell the difference.'

'Maybe her near-death experience made her realize what she's been missing, eh? Wink, wink, nudge, nudge,' smiled Paul.

'Maybe... but,' TJ said absently before he realized what had been said, 'What?'

'You know the size of your blade,' he snickered, 'and how well you wield it.'

'Shut up, man!' TJ smiled.

Kain was still laughing at his own joke even after TJ pushed him over and he hit the ground, reflexively clutching his sides. Everyone kept on walking as Kain rolled on the ground. Iceman and Duke sidestepped Kain with big grins on their faces. After a minute or so the laughter spasms eased and allowed Kain to get up. He ran to catch up with TJ again.

'Are you quite done?' TJ asked with a half-amused grin.

'Yeah, eh; yeah, sorry TJ,' he said with a hint of laughter still in his voice.

'That was nice,' Buzz chuckled.

TJ stole quick glance over his shoulder and across the convoy to where Daniella was talking with Amanda. Unfortunately for TJ, that was the same moment Daniella and Amanda chose to glance over at him. This produced a few giggles, not as many, however as when TJ snapped his head forwards again. Even the seemingly forever silent Blademaster, Ann Huston cracked a smile as she followed behind the women.

They all marched in relative silence for the remainder of the five-hour excursion that brought them half way to where the squad had last been attacked. They had no intention of walking into a trap so they began to steer away from that site. This did not mean they were going to clear the hills – far from it.

The western part of the Brossan Hills was both deeper and steeper than the direct path to Fort Saturn. The added wind block of the hills in this region made for a perfect environment for denser brush, narrowing their marching order. For their first night, they made camp at the base of the cliff which signalled the southern-most end of the hills. The large BRAT pulled up parallel to the cliff-face and came to a rest about two yards away. The other vehicles fanned out from its position in a perfectly even semi-circle.

They built a fire at the centre of the camp, more out of habit than necessity. The BRAT would serve as the medical vehicle as well as carrying and providing the food for everyone, a big change from hauling cargo like it used to do. It had been retrofitted with a matter-energy converter to synthesize its new catering operation.

The commanding officers set out a shift schedule almost as soon as the sleds settled on the grass with four troopers standing watch at all times. For added protection one of the four would be a Blademaster. First watch went out shortly after dusk for a three-hour shift. The rest of the two squads sat and talked about the days to come or milled about. Four of the group rested for their shift.

'What are we guarding against exactly?' the newly added First Recon trooper, Cathy Calara asked.

'You were briefed on the situation out here, Cathy,' Daniella said.

'Oh, I know the official story, but I think we deserve to know the truth. You don't even know what hit you, Daniella.'

'Yeah, she's right. What gives?' Vance Parski, another rookie spoke up. He retained the arrogant athletic-type attitude from high school that still tended to grind on people.

'Whoa, relax,' Marsha Brown, the Second Recon addition broke in.

'Oh, hush up everyone,' Dolly said, 'We'll tell you the *true* story, Okay?'

'Whatever you heard in the briefing,' Erik Krushell paused, 'that's what is out there. They're real, you monkeys! I saw them! I burnt out a blade fighting them off so they wouldn't drag us away for food!'

'Easy Erik,' Daniella soothed.

'But it sounds like...' Erik started.

'You did good kid, let it go,' Kain put in. Erik's eyes almost popped out of his head and his jaw tried to fall through his suit when he heard the words of praise from the Blademaster.

'So why don't we have any pictures or footage of some kind?' Dallas Cooper, new Second Recon stepped in, 'you say this and that and we're supposed to take your word for it?'

'Damn right,' Buzz said calmly, 'Whether true or not this is the militia and they are your commanding officers so it falls on you to do what they say and believe what they tell you.'

'You want pictures?' snapped TJ, 'I lost four good troopers and a GCR to these things. If you need proof so badly, then look at their bodies. I'll show you a burned-out wreck of a GCR right now. These things are real and if you aren't ready when they come, I'll be dragging your dead ass back to Fort Grey and calling your folks. You clear, soldier?'

That pretty much ended the conversation for the night right there. Nights were always dark on the peninsula with the haze blocking out all light from the stars and the lack of a moon in orbit. Tonight seemed to get a little darker within the camp. Slowly, everyone made his or her way to a comfortable place to bed down and await the coming of the next day.

*****

CHAPTER VII
Tuesday, 4 April, 2251

The uneventful night changed into the hustle and bustle of the early hours of the morning. The plan was to break camp one hour after sunrise to optimize their travel times under the sun. Too much activity occupied the members of the convoy for them to enjoy the sunrise and welcome it to the world as they normally would have. Troopers and officers alike hurried about the campsite loading the BRAT with the equipment used during the night. The last watch of the night slept in the gunner seats of the four GCRs, which allowed them to become fully rested.

The two squads formed up for this day's march in much the same fashion as the day before. The difference in today's parade was the high level of tension. No one talked above a whisper and there was no laughing today. To avoid another possible ambush the team had veered to the west of the usual route taken to Fort Saturn. There was no time to marvel at the new land they were found, having now crossed out of the charted part of the peninsula. Instead all eyes were on the fuzzy green haze of horizon and the visible land as it shifted from hill crest to valley floor. Hills would appear out of the haze almost as if they were only then being drawn. There was no evidence they would encounter the gargoyle-things again but past experience with the ambush at the wreck site taught them to expect anything so their blades and cannons were a moment from action.

The group marched through the hills, keeping mainly to the valleys between which felt like covered tunnels even under the light of both the yellow and blue suns. A hurried pace was maintained so they could cross these dreaded hills as quickly as possible. Whatever was on the north-western side had to be better than this unpredictable terrain. No one knew what technology these creatures possessed, although the general impression was any enhancement of their abilities over their already impressive power was a bad thing.

The troops marched quickly and uneasily for six hours before Major Harte ordered a scouting unit to crest the hill to the north. The hill was currently sheltering them from a brisk wind welling up from the north, but she intended to go over anyway rather than around. Amanda's visibility was less than a half mile to start with until these hills cut that to less than one hundred yards – she was getting edgy. The unit she sent consisted of a GCR and four troopers. As they crested the hill, rain started to dampen their already low spirits. It started as a shower but they knew rain on the Eden peninsula quickly turned into a downpour and were always accompanied by wind... not good.

Environmental conditions mattered little to the power armour as it had been designed to withstand much worse than a spot of rain. However, as always, weather had an effect on the human mind and heart inside that same armour. The troopers were tense as they watched the scouts advance to the north while they sheltered themselves under a large-branched coniferous tree growth running the length of the south hill. These tall, blue-tinted trees filled the valley only on the north side of the hills and provided little shelter from the south blowing rain.

Looking from the micro-summit with his suit's vision enhancement equipment, Peter Davies could see for a thousand yards in every direction with the help of the crystal-shift phenomenon that could act as a magnifying glass. It was an amazing phenomenon that worked great if you were looking for something but horrible if you tried to gauge the distance. To the south towards the rest of the squad, were hills and a few groves of trees poking out of the valleys. To the west and north, the hills gradually became smaller and eventually faded into lush dark-green fields.

To the north, he thought he could barely make out the brilliant red of the Comb Plateau, the only major landmark on the peninsula, though the chances of him actually seeing it was remote. Its sheer cliffs rose as high as four thousand feet in some places. Below the south-eastern edge of the plateau was the settlement of Fort Saturn, a bustling settlement of five thousand or more by now. Even though he could not see the marvellous city, he knew it was there. Call it a hometown instinct. He was one of the few troopers in this march that had seen more of the world than the four points of Fort Grey.

To the east, Peter could barely see a small, faint shape looking like an overturned spider. Though it was almost a mile away from him, he thought he could see wisps of smoke rising from the shape. It was probably an illusion since they must be a dozen miles away from the reported site and what were the chances there was another wrecked GCR?

'We're almost out of the hills,' Peter shouted over the now thundering rain. Sparkling drops of rain beat on the armour with little effect but the hit still registered as impacts to the suit's onboard computer.

'Good,' shouted Steve in return, 'I've almost forgotten what flat ground looks like!'

'Let's just get back to the others so we can get out of this rain,' Rich Jarvis replied. He was a Blademaster from the Second Recon. Even though he was warm and dry, he shuddered visibly. Thunder boomed overhead adding a punctuation mark to the statement.

'Good idea,' Viper said.

'What do you know, lady? You're sitting in the GCR,' Marsha snapped.

'So are you, Marsha,' Erik laughed. Everyone broke the tension as they laughed with him.

'I'll call back our findings,' Steve said after he had recovered.

'Okay,' Viper said automatically.

'Wait!' Peter screamed.

It was too late to stop the transmission. Steve's signal had already gone out. All the heads in the valley swivelled around to glare up the hill. The scouting group had all stopped in their tracks and were silhouetted against a rapidly darkening sky.

'What?' Steve asked.

'Radio silence, you dolt!' Marsha shouted.

'What's the big deal? We haven't seen a soul in a day and a half. I don't think anyone could hear us if we set off a cannon.'

'Yeah, I guess maybe you're right. But I think…' Viper started.

An eerily familiar shriek arose above the sounds of the storm from the east and south. Instantly, all eyes at the top of the hill started to scan the sky. Then to the southeast, dark specks seen against the bright band of sky under the leading edge of the clouds jumped into the air with emerald green light pulsing on both sides of each of them.

'It can't be!' Steve said, stunned.

'Run!' Viper shouted, 'Back to the convoy!'

'Lieutenant, we got incoming!' Rich broadcasted as he ran down the hill. It seemed illogical to remain under radio silence now.

'Everyone get ready! Duke, Rich, you watch over the beam cannons. Everyone else, light 'em up!' Amanda ordered.

The convoy was at their optimum readiness for battle within seconds. The Blademasters Duke and Rich positioned themselves on either side of the two heavy-weapon specialists, ready for anything that may get through. The entire convoy was backing their way up the valley, still heading northwest. There was no sign of the gargoyles but they knew they were nearby.

'What set them off?' Daniella asked.

'I sent a transmission to Fort Grey, but there's no way they could have heard it,' Steve said.

'What on Mars did you do that for? The Fort doesn't need to hear that stuff! There was no need to transmit long range,' Buzz exclaimed.

'They must be able to hear or sense long distance transmissions,' TJ said.

'But they're just stupid animals,' Steve cried.

'Guess not, bud,' Dolly said without looking at him.

When they next looked, gargoyles appeared on the eastern and southern hills but kept their distance, as if studying. Their wings remained lit over the ones beside each of them as if providing shelter from the rain while they watched. The grass was slick in the rain but the convoy managed to continue through to the edge northward slowly with everyone alert, watching for any sign of an impending attack. The demonic forms paced the convoy but remained on the ridge crests out of range. Both groups continued to observe, the humans not wanting to get in a fight considering their poor tactical location and the gargoyles apparently looking for any weakness. The valley began to bank towards the west, away from a potential battleground and away from the distant safety of Fort Saturn.

'We're deviating west, Major!' Buzz called after a moment.

'We'll have to go over the hill,' Amanda announced.

'Carefully everyone and no sudden movements!' TJ added.

Cathy, Denyse and Steve were in the lead group cutting through the foliage and were the first to crest the hill, and the first to stop dead in their tracks. In the valley, on the north side of the hill, were easily fifty or sixty gargoyles, silent and waiting. The soldiers had not been seen yet, thankfully. They slowly turned around and stepped back carefully towards the convoy, which by now, had stopped. Scanning the hills, Buzz began to register signals not conforming to the landscape, it was apparent that they were completely surrounded. TJ made his way to the trio.

'We're hooped sir,' Denyse muttered. Waving an arm back the way they had come.

'Why, what's over there?' TJ asked.

'More of them, sir. Lots more,' Cathy said.

'And we're surrounded,' Steve said indicating the hills around them. Hunched figures with glowing green eyes appeared in an almost continuous line around them, 'I'm sorry guys. I didn't think.'

'That's right, you didn't,' TJ put in, 'but now is not the time for self-pity, trooper.'

TJ scanned the hills with eyes and sensors to get the best picture. There were at least twenty maybe thirty creatures on the eastern hills with more on the way, undoubtedly. There were fifteen to twenty gargoyles in position on the hills to the south and another fifteen or so on the western side.

'Okay, I'm guessing these animals know basic tactics at least, they know about herding anyway. I want you three to do exactly as I say, and when I say it, got it!'

'Yes sir,' all three chimed in.

'Now, when I give the signal, I want you to run down this hill and head southwest. Maybe we can circle around to Fort Grey,' TJ said, 'Ready... go!'

TJ cranked up his signal output, 'This is Lieutenant Marso of the Second Recon squad to all units within the sound of my voice,' The entire convoy stopped what they were doing and turned to look at TJ, 'the First and Second Recon squads, Fort Grey division are under attack by over one hundred alien life forms. We are heading southwest from the Brossan Hills in an attempt to circle back to Fort Grey. All other units are ordered to stay away from this area.'

The four of them raced past the momentarily stunned convoy heading northwest. A shriek from the gargoyles around them snapped their paralysis and they moved in right behind TJ. At the sight of the charging convoy, the creatures surrounding them reacted. Their wings lit up as they converged on the group and green fire spewed from their arms as they ignited their arm blades. All the blades in the two squads came to life, vaporizing the rain with a crackling hiss as the micro-shards destroyed the atomic connections in the drops. As TJ came to the top of the hill and parted the last bush on the rise, eight gargoyles appeared in front of him. He had no time to think of another way around. Fortunately, his reactions and those of the convoy made up for the lack of problem solving.

The gargoyle to his immediate left fell to the ground with a grunt as a brilliant blue beam from a heavy weapons specialist sliced through it from the centre of its sternum to its left shoulder. The creature to his right ended its existence as another similar beam burned a large steaming hole straight through its head. A gargoyle that had jumped into the air for a killing down-stroke was blasted into so much fertilizer by two double-wide blinding blue beams from the BRAT. The beams were much hotter than the operating temperature of the blade consequently there was almost no blood from the falling bodies and fragments of the victims.

Similar beams blazed from the GCRs, cutting down the next four adversaries. Various body parts were vaporized or cleanly severed. The last gargoyle, which had stood directly in front of TJ, had no time to react with his companions disappearing and falling around him. TJ's blade severed the left forearm of the gargoyle, knocking the useless limb out of the way. He spun around quickly and brought his blade up and under the creature's right arm, through and out to the left of the neck. TJ kept on running with the convoy, letting the rain wash away the splatters of green blood on his armour

The group surged over the hill and the fallen gargoyles and into a valley leading straight out of the hills to the open fields of the south peninsula. They reached the valley floor seconds before the first of the pursuing creatures appeared behind them. The first two over the hill met the same fate as those that had tried to stop the humans, shattering as the deadly beams creased the sky.

After a short pause in the activity, the remaining body of the gargoyle blockade flooded in from three sides. The haze and the storm surrounding the convoy pulsated with a dull-green pulsing light heralding the approach of the alien army. Beam cannons howled as soon as a target emerged from the haze and cut down a dozen or more as they rapidly came into range. Shot after shot from the GCRs lit the skies over the valley with a rhythm seemingly in time with lightning bursts. The gargoyles moved in fast, catching the human convoy in seconds. Blades met forearm scythes shortly after in a light show resembling a photo shoot.

Cathy Calara was the first human to fall, taking five gargoyles with her when a scythe ripped through her micro-reactor, causing a small fusion detonation.

Daylight returned to the field of battle for a few seconds when the bright orange-yellow blast sprang to life. The blast wave incinerated the first four gargoyles around her and knocked about ten others well back. The fifth casualty was knocked back by the shockwave into a beam aimed at another gargoyle and was sliced in half.

No less than a dozen gargoyles descended from the north and latched onto the lead GCR, tearing it to shreds. Blue-white energy bolts started shooting out from the sled seconds before its reactor when critical. Fortunately for Viper, the pilot, she managed to hit her *eject* button before the sled went up. The explosive bolts for the escape hatch blew the hatch off perfectly and also blasted one of the attacking creatures into a fine green mist.

The instant before she left, however, she had turned the crippled sled into the main enemy group. When the sled went up the explosion was so massive, it took with it the gunner, Marsha, and almost two-dozen gargoyles. Viper landed and rolled to her feet a few feet in front of the heavy weapon fire team.

'Everyone get on a vehicle, we need to get out of here... now!' Amanda cried as the gargoyle in front of her fell to the ground.

The squad jumped on to the tactical rails on the sides of the GCRs and the BRAT as the vehicles accelerated to the top speed of forty miles-per-hour. The speed was almost beyond what the armour could resist, crystal haze pressed hard against them like trying to move through water. The gargoyles seemed to be built for this kind of weather and managed to match their speed, if not actually overtaking them. With the troopers hanging on the sides and standing on the tops, the beam cannons were not able to fire without hitting their own people. This provided the gargoyles with an advantage and they knew it and zoomed in closer.

'Peter, look out!' yelled Erik from the left side of the GCR now in the lead. The warning was too late, two gargoyles pulled him off to the right side. His blade sliced at them, severing one's head from the rest of its body. With Peter gone from the beam cannon's sights, Buzz fired before four more gargoyles descended on the trooper and tagged at least one of them. No one actually saw what happened next to the unlucky trooper, though his screams could be heard briefly on the internal speakers before the roar of the rain and sounds of battle drowned it out.

Half a dozen gargoyles jumped onto the BRAT to engage the riders. Their wings closed against their backs but their arms and eyes flared in anticipation of battle. A beam shot out from Iceman's cannon, cutting through a gargoyle's wing at a sharp angle and creasing its back. Before the stream of light made its way to the crippling hit, a second gargoyle jumped from behind its companion, wings blazing green and the same deadly colour as its eyes.

'Die human!' it growled as it surged forward. Its massive fangs made the words rumble out but the message was clear.

'Holy...' started Iceman but was quickly cut off as the last foot of his cannon was severed by a forearm scythe and fell off the BRAT. A second beast swung at his head before he could detach his harness but was interrupted by Duke's blade.

'Don't count your chickens, friend,' Ann Huston snapped from the left side of the creature as she brought her blade through the jumping creature's shoulder. She turned from her victim and kicked the wing-wounded gargoyle off the BRAT. They noticed Steve was fighting three gargoyles near the left rear of the BRAT and was almost dragged off to an unspeakable end before Rich stepped in. He managed to cripple one with a slash to the back of the leg, kill another and knock the third off the side before a fourth gargoyle tackled him sending both he and the hellish thing over the edge of the machine. Without thinking, Steve went over after Rich and vanished into the storm and haze. Howls from the dying gargoyles could be heard over the rush of the driving wind and rain. The constant wind was a factor of the battle no one had been paying much attention to, even though it was one of the most important factors to travel on the Eden peninsula. Upon looking at his instrument panel in the lead GCR, Buzz realized the convoy was being pushed west, despite its efforts to go south. He also noticed the patterns were shifting drastically. That could mean only one thing... a major storm was coming.

One of the most dreaded things on Mars was a storm system. Ten years ago, a violent storm ripped apart the McNess Research facility, located on the southwest end of the peninsula. Fortunately, as of late the powerful storms were mainly out on the oceans. By the looks of the dark swirls of cloud gathering overhead, this one was going to be nasty.

'Lieutenant!' Buzz shouted, 'We've got a massive thunder-boomer headed our way. The winds are picking up.'

TJ surveyed the skies and glanced at the horizon now blending together. No pulsing wings from the gargoyles could be seen in the navy-coloured sky or along the heavily rain-washed ground. Lightning pulsed in the distance, occasionally turning the dark of reality into the light of fantasy. Shadows pulsed up everywhere, and spooked troopers twirled anxiously to meet foes that were not there.

'Are you sure about that? What are you reading, Dolly?' TJ asked, 'Storms don't usually come this far inland.'

'Buzz is right, I mean, that's the thing, sir,' said Ken. He really did not like being called Dolly, especially on the public band wave. 'We're only about six hundred yards from the coast. The wind has been pushing us really fast. We are, however, due south of Fort Saturn.'

'Well, thank the light for that,' Kain muttered.

'Damn, we'll have to dig in here.'

'What!' Major Harte snapped, 'We'll do no such thing, Lieutenant! Those things will be on us in a second. We have to keep moving! West, if we have to.'

The little GCRs wobbled now and then as the ever-increasing winds pummelled them. Their wind deflection wings could do little to compensate for the violent shifting gales. 'If we stay up, we'll be tossed into the sea. Major, we have to put down,' TJ said firmly.

'Negative! We'll look for cover away from those blasted hills.'

'This area hasn't even been mapped yet, Major. We don't know what's out here let alone if there's shelter,' Buzz said from the number one GCR.

'We are on an incline now, ma'am,' Chuck hollered from the sled he was piloting.

'If I remember correctly The Sky Trees should be coming up soon then,' Viper put in.

'How do you know that?' Buzz called back.

'I think I read a report about forestry and mining locations.'

'What were you doin.... Never mind. That's the best idea we've got,' TJ said.

'Get there, then,' Amanda ordered.

The convoy surged forward into the storm racing from darkness to a different darkness. While the large and heavy BRAT was only slightly affected by the buffeting of the fierce winds, the little GCRs were being pounded back and forth. At one point, within visual range of the first of the massive Sky Trees, a pair of wind deflection wings broke off the sled piloted by Vance and he lost control. TJ, Kain and Viper, who had been riding on the outside until that point, were all thrown off and were tumbled through the mud. The GCR careened through the convoy to the left, forcing the BRAT to veer hard to the right to avoid a collision.

Daniella, Amanda, Ann, Iceman and Duke were all dumped unceremoniously on top of TJ's group causing more than a few dents in the armour and egos. The BRAT slid to a halt at a forty-five degree angle to the path of travel, which allowed it to act as a wind block. The crew of the sled had no time to jump free before the little vehicle was hurtled over the edge of the cliff into the turbulent, night time seawater more than one hundred feet below.

'Damn,' TJ whispered from his squat position against the hull of the BRAT.

'Who was that?' Daniella asked.

'Vance and Larry,' Brian Sternik, the executive officer of the First Recon said.

'I told you we should have dug in.'

'I know what I'm doing, TJ,' Amanda snapped as she struggled to control her emotion, 'That was an unfortunate incident. The storm is getting worse. We'll have to take cover.'

'Let's do as the Major says, boys and girls. The trees are just up ahead,' TJ ordered with more than a little contempt in his voice.

'You watch your tone, mister!' Amanda snapped, 'I've warned you before, and if it happens again I'll have you locked up regardless of any fighting ahead. Am I clear, Lieutenant?'

'Crystal, ma'am,' TJ saluted.

*****

CHAPTER VIII
Wednesday, 5 April, 2251

Dawn came to the Sky Trees at D130 hours, with Sol peeking through the cloud cover and a sparse section of the canopy from the direction of Fort Grey. With dawn came the promise of a new day, though not necessarily a better day. The results of the past night were clearly visible in the pale grey of the morning light.

TJ and Duke had taken the last watch of the night, allowing them to be the first to survey the damage done to the two squads. They started the roll call to determine the extent of the losses the squads had suffered.

Sleeping troopers lay between the BRAT and the two remaining GCRs. Their armour was in poor condition. Those whose armour escaped scorching, cuts or denting beyond field repair were so caked with heavy, damp mud from the rainfall last night they almost completely blended into the ground they lay upon. While the canopy was patchy in the leafy coverage the undergrowth was impassable save for a few oddly wide wildlife trails.

The vehicles were another matter. It was immediately clear how close they had come to a violent end, similar to Marsha's fate. It was also painfully obvious their efforts to keep the gargoyles at bay were not near as successful as they had thought.

Large gouges were present along all sides of the three remaining vehicles, most prominent on the BRAT. On closer inspection, TJ noticed puncture holes and ripped plating on the side and rear armour plates of the GCRs, almost as if the creatures were trying to chew their way inside. He decided to not initiate a wave of panic, keeping the information to himself.

At D215 hours with both stars now in the sky, TJ and Duke roused those troopers who had not already begun to stir. Slowly, with groans from aching muscles and a few coarse words from interrupted dreams, the men and the women of the First and Second Recon Squads lifted themselves up for another day of probable hell.

'Sir,' called the last trooper TJ had kicked from what looked to be a rather uncomfortable position. He was lying on his back on the ground, not moving an inch since the contact with TJ's boot.

'What is it, Trooper…' TJ paused, 'Dean isn't it?'

'Yes, sir,' Dean's voice was muffled by his armour, 'I can't seem...'

'You'll have to speak up, man. Turn your speakers on.'

'I can't sir,' there was considerable strain in his voice as the armoured figure shook while trying to sit up, 'I... think my armour's dead.' His slightly vibrating form slumped back into the depression he had left in the ground from lying there all night.

'Buzz,' TJ called to his XO, who was stepping out of the BRAT with his breakfast in hand.

Buzz was still banged up, even though he had spent yesterday in one of the GCRs. The wind buffeting the sled, knocking him around inside had done most of the damage to his armour. The younger officer was perky as always, although showing signs of fatigue despite a full night's rest.

'Come over here. We need to get Mr. Kosh here, into the BRAT so that Johnny can get a good look at his suit.'

'Sure, chief; no problem,' replied Bill as he walked to Dean's right side, bending down to lift.

'One, two three – pull!'

'I think it's diet time, private,' Buzz joked. The trooper was popped out of the dark red mud.

They managed to pull Dean free of the mud with a surprising amount of effort, lifting the six hundred pounds of man and machine up onto his feet. Once up, with Buzz's help to steady the living mummy, TJ stole a quick glance at the power pack on Dean's back.

The front of the armour suit was only slightly dented from the ride in the cab of the BRAT the night before and was almost sparkling clean. The rear of his armour pack was another matter. There was a gash, maybe two feet long, perfectly vertical, down the middle of the pack.

Although the slice had narrowly missed the two reactors powering the suit, the attack had cleanly severed the lower reactant-transfer line. The suit would have lost power sometime in the middle of the night, trapping the trooper in the mud. TJ's mind flashbacked to Marshal's armour freezing up instantly the gargoyle's scythe had passed through both upper and lower transfer lines. He had a second flash of seeing Cathy's reactors go critical as a scythe had most likely cut horizontally through both the fission and fusion reactors.

'Boy, you is one lucky bastard.'

Dolly whistled when he viewed the damage.

Ken's remark snapped TJ back to the present.

'Yeah, Ken is right, Dean. You almost went crit! Buzz, you and Ken get him into the BRAT. I have something to check.'

'Are we sure he won't still blow?' Buzz asked, half joking.

TJ stared after the trio for a moment. He made his way down the side of the transport to the control cabin of the BRAT. The left side of the cab was untouched by anything more violent than a tree branch. The damage to Dean's pack had not come from this side. He stood for a moment, trying to reason what could have occurred. How could a trooper's armour be so badly damaged while sitting inside an armoured vehicle?

The hit could not have come from the rear because the cargo area was not penetrated with a hole large enough to let a gargoyle through, a hit in the front of the cabin could not have hit the trooper's pack, meaning the right side must have been compromised.

TJ walked around the front of the BRAT to the right side, stunned at the extent of the damage. A cut in the plating in the shape of a square was almost like a door the size a gargoyle would need to get in. Peering into the slice, TJ could see into the interior of the cabin through the ruined communication terminal attached to the wall.

Aside from the sheer magnitude of the damage, something else bothered TJ about the scene. He had witnessed the cutting action of the scythes first hand and figured it was impossible those he saw could have cut deep enough. The only thing he knew that could cut through that much equipment, was a blade.

This left him with three possible events – first, some new technology had done the damage, second, someone in the group of people was aiding the creatures, or these strange animals were using blades likely taken from the convoy, as would a human.

'Oh, shit,' TJ whispered.

'Hey! There's a hole in the side of the BRAT,' Chuck cried.

'Oh, really,' TJ mocked, 'you think?'

'Oh yeah, definitely sir. It's right there.' Chuck pointed out the damage.

'Thanks trooper,' TJ sighed. He had obviously missed the sarcasm. 'Look, all we can do is close up that hole before we set out again and see if the console can be repaired.'

'But sir, I can't fix electronics.'

'I didn't mean... listen, just maybe you could get someone who can fix electronics,' he said, pausing, '...like maybe Brian or Johnny.' TJ turned and walked away from the transport and Chuck before any rebuttal. With absolutely no faith the damage would be repaired, he needed to find Amanda.

TJ finally found Amanda talking to Ann and Daniella on a small rise which offered a pleasant view towards the ocean, somehow disbelieving they were close enough to see the sea. It was an amazing sight he had never seen before but the situation was too tense to stop and admire the rolling purple waves. From the hill, it was clear the group had penetrated the forest farther west than they had estimated.

Although not his intention, he approached the three unnoticed. The sound of hurried footsteps behind TJ finally drew their attention. TJ turned towards the footsteps before the women turned towards him, making it difficult to identify him. That his armour was in no better condition than the other troopers made it even harder. Amanda and Ann gave a start at the armoured figure standing not more than twenty feet from them, while Daniella smiled, even though she too was surprised.

'What do you want, trooper?' Amanda addressed TJ.

'Trooper?' asked an amused TJ as he grabbed the arm of the soldier behind him to steady him after his run up the hill. 'What is it, Erik?'

'Sorry to disturb you sir, but we've found another problem.'

'Lovely, what is it this time?'

'The reactor in GCR-Two is dead.' Erik was panting, obviously his armour was low on power reserves.

'How?' asked TJ. 'It was working at sunrise.'

'Just after you left to come up here, we heard a hiss and a pop. That was it sir, no reactor and a tidy hole in the side plating.'

'What's the matter, TJ?' Major Harte asked. She found herself smiling, she had never been on a field op before and never on any operation with TJ. Seeing him work through the events of last night was amazing. This mission showed him in a new light. He was assertive, a man of action, nothing like the slacker she had taken him for.

'Thanks, Erik,' TJ turned back to the women, 'Looks like I've got three things to report now.' Daniella was still smiling at him. He shifted his weight to look more relaxed, which he was not.

When he saw Amanda's smile he shifted the other way.

'Okay then, first,' Amanda said.

'It seems that one of your boys took what could have been a fatal shot in last night's action ... Koch.'

'Dean?' Daniella was confused, '... but he was in the BRAT!'

'Yeah, it looks like either one of us or one of those things used a blade to cut through the side of the cab.'

'By the Light! Is he okay?'

'Yeah, it just diced his power supply pretty good but he's alright. I've got one of my guys patching his suit right now and another hopefully patching the BRAT.'

'Fine. Second item is...' Amanda asked. She did not like bad news on her watch and now she was getting multiple bad reports.

'Oh, sorry, that was the second,' said TJ, 'hole in your boy and a blade punctured the BRAT and it all means we can't leave for another hour.'

'An hour! But we have t...' Amanda was not happy with the report or the mission for that matter, 'Fine. How do you figure that a blade was used?'

'Because, ma'am, I just don't think that the scythes on their forearms can reach as far as the damage indicates. Which means...'

'Which means we have a turn-coat in our midst,' Ann cut in.

'Actually, I was about to say that the gargoyles know how to use our blades.'

'That's impossible, they're just animals,' Daniella said.

'Everything I've seen about these creatures tells me they aren't just animals. They adapt and they're cunning. They use tactics of long-time hunters. And they use strategies we would use in a war.'

'You're saying that they're intelligent, aren't you?' Amanda asked.

'That's what it looks like to me.'

'Okay, let me think on this a while,' she said, putting a hand to her helmet, the other on her hip. 'What's number three?'

'A little oddity that Erik just told me. It appears someone has disabled one of the GCRs. The reactor's dead.'

'Oh, for the...' Amanda took a deep breath, 'How, TJ? There's like twenty or so trained men and women buzzing around down there, how on Mars could they disable a GCR?'

'Sabotage!' Ann said.

'It sounds like someone fired a beam cannon into the fusion reactor and the safeties cut in.'

'Wonderful!' Amanda sighed. 'Any theories?'

'Not yet,' TJ replied.

'Let's just go down and get things moving. I don't want to be any later to Fort Saturn than we already are. Daniella, TJ, try to have the units ready to roll by D300 hours.'

'Yes, ma'am,' they replied in unison.

By D245 hours, the supplies stored in the disabled GCR had been divided and transferred to the remaining GCR and BRAT. A new armour plate was laser-welded in place over the *door* the gargoyles had tried to cut into the side of the BRAT. The gap in Dean's armour was repaired and the power system of his suit was recharged. The troop was ready to move out, though not excited.

The five senior officers stood next to the crippled GCR discussing the route to be taken. They formed a triangle with TJ and Buzz of the Second Recon leaning on the side of the GCR, Daniella and Brian of the First Recon to the left. Amanda stood at the point between the two command elements while Ann stood behind her, out of the conversation, looking ready to step in at any moment.

TJ glanced over at Ann, 'Does she have to be here? I was under the impression that this kind of thing was for ranking field officers only,' he said to Daniella.

'Relax, TJ,' she said putting a hand on his arm, 'Ann is just Amanda's protection, a bodyguard if you like.'

'Protection from what?'

'You saw how fast those things jumped us yesterday,' Amanda added. She did not know why she was frowning at Daniella's hand on his arm, 'Commander Martel was insistent I make it to Fort Saturn. So, the best ways to ensure my safety is to have a Blademaster watch my back.'

'Fine,' TJ conceded, 'let's get back to business then.'

'Right. We're currently seventy-five miles west and one hundred and thirty miles south of Fort Saturn, near as I can figure it anyway. I don't want to risk trying to link up with positioning radar in case those things can track that too,' Brian said.

'There's at least a mile of forest to the east and a whole lot more to the north,' Buzz added.

'Right, then we should make our way east-northeast. That way we can get out on to open terrain and then make a beeline to Fort Saturn.'

'They'll be expecting that,' Buzz said.

'What?' asked Daniella, 'Who?'

'The gargoyles, they'll know we'll try to leave the trees. They'll know, I tell you!'

'I think Buzz is right,' TJ said, putting his hand on Buzz's shoulder to calm him down. 'With what we've seen so far, I have to agree with him.'

'Then what, TJ? You want us to go through the trees?' Daniella asked, her smile slipping away.

'Yeah actually, that is exactly what I think we should do, Lieutenant Klon. I've lost half a dozen troopers and a lot of equipment to these things and I don't feel like losing any more. Daniella, you've lost over a dozen people. They've ambushed us twice so far. Let's not play into their hands again. The trees give us cover, let's use it.'

'I think maybe TJ's right, Amanda, we should go through the forest. That way we may even lose them and have a relatively easy trip to Fort Saturn.'

'I'm sure I won't like it, but if you two agree then we'll give it a go,' Amanda smiled at Daniella being taken down a notch, 'Tell the troops that we leave in ten minutes.'

'Ten minutes? We can't get underway in only...' TJ protested.

'Just do it, TJ!' she snapped.

'Yes, ma'am,' TJ replied.

'Yes, ma'am,' Daniella saluted.

As everyone was departing for his or her positions, TJ pulled Daniella aside, 'Daniella, I'm sorry I snapped at you back there. I just don't like surprises, especially in the field and most definitely when it involves these things.'

'It's okay, TJ,' she said softly, 'I know you're just concerned about your people and mine.'

'Yeah,' he said, 'and thanks for siding with me to convince Amanda. I didn't want a big hassle with her.'

'You seemed to have got one anyway,' she smiled.

'Just a little one. Thanks again, Daniella.'

'You're welcome, babe, um... TJ,' she blushed and ran off to her place in the convoy.

*****

Commander Martel set down the report handed to him by the Communications chief. His desk was starting to show disarray. In the report was the communiqué from Major Harte's group informing him they were clearing the Brossan Hills. It was odd they would radio in to report, unless there was some doubt as to whether they could make it. It did not sit easy with him.

Could it be that more of those things had attacked them? They had been gone for two days and in that time there had been no contacts beyond the walls. Patrols had been out and they had come back without as much as a scratch.

'Captain Ladore,' he said to the officer who had handed the report to him. 'Have we been able to contact Major Harte since the transmission?'

'No, sir,' she replied. 'We've been trying every half hour since the initial communication, but I am confident we will be able to break through the interference.'

'Do we know what is causing it yet?'

'It seems to be a local disruption. A boost to the outer rim relay tower should be enough.'

'Okay, thank you Captain.' The trooper saluted and turned to leave. Commander Martel looked briefly out his window to the inner walkway of the fort before moving to signal the on-deck squad. 'Lieutenant Carken,' he started, thumbing the intercom for the North Barracks CO, 'I want...'

'Commander!' an urgent voice broke in, 'We have several contacts closing on our location. Rate of travel is approximately fifty miles-per-hour. We've already lost the outer relay tower.'

'Sound the Level Three alert. How many do we have?' Commander Martel felt his heart drop. This cannot be happening to his people!

'Fifty to seventy contacts, sir!' The young man shouted over the wail of the alert, adding, '... and their numbers appear to be increasing.'

'Damn!' Martel closed the channel and opened the general address system. 'Attention, this is Commander Martel. All personnel are to report to their battle stations. Gunner crews, get to your turrets. Repeat! Battle stations!'

The contacts registering on the scope closed the distance to Fort Grey with remarkable speed and far faster than he had anticipated. Even so the remaining five combat squads, as well as any non-combat personnel, were armed and ready for battle; in total, over five hundred people were in the path of these things.

In theory, seventy gargoyles should be no match for that number of humans in a fortified structure. A number of things were sure to go wrong, he thought; there were always bound to be some glitches involved when things looked too easy.

'They appear to be approaching from due northwest. Only one of the cannons can hit them,' said a civilian aide to Commander Martel in the Strategy Room.

'That's one,' Martel said to himself.

'Sir?' the aide queried.

'In any combat situation there will be things that go wrong, young man. It's okay, as long as there are no more than one or two. After that the battle becomes a free-for-all and plans go out the window. And that,' he indicated the only firing arc on the map, 'is the first.'

There was a sudden, thunderous hum from the fort's massive northwest class-7 cannon, announcing the creatures' arrival. The blast took four of the airborne gargoyles by surprise, turning them into a fine glowing green mist. The second shot caught two gargoyles that were too slow to dodge the beam, dividing the creatures cleanly across the midsection.

Still the gargoyles came, quickly in range of the vehicle and portable beam cannons. The vehicles were in a line between the north and west points of Fort Grey's walls. The dozen armoured civilian and military men and women along with half a dozen GCRs stood at the bend of the wall behind the beam turret.

Beams of dazzling blue, emerald and ruby blazed through the sky and caught several gargoyles in a deadly crossfire. In the blaze of light a beam deflected off a scythe instead of taking off the arm of the lucky gargoyle. The creatures abruptly changed tactics now that they saw what you could do with the beams. The next shot from a vehicle was neatly blocked by the target and deflected into the ground beside the firing vehicle.

Commander Martel saw the intentional deflection from the control room, 'That's number two,' he said grimly.

The fort's beam cannon had its next shot deflected. The gargoyle doing the deflecting was itself vaporized but enough of the shot was redirected. The rebounded shot punched through the turret's armour and detonated the tiny reactor powering the weapon.

As two hundred cubic yards of air, personnel and fort superstructure was incinerated, all Martel could say was, '... and that, is number three.'

The battle had raged for less than an hour and already it looked bad. When the wall had been breached, four hundred of the civilians in the fort compound, who had not been armoured or equipped with air filters, were rendered effectively useless and they were quickly slaughtered. In the last half an hour, almost twenty troopers had fallen. The gargoyles had lost forty or fifty of their numbers but the difference in this equation was they seemed to have received double that number in re-enforcements.

'How does it look, Sergeant?' Martel asked.

'The north barracks and west medical wings have been taken, sir. We've got maybe thirty troopers holed up in the vehicle bay and forty-five of us here in the command bunker and south barracks.'

'Our forces seem to have been completely divided, sir,' another said. 'They're using the blades from the civvies they slaughtered and they're advancing.'

'Let's go then, one final hurrah, eh?' Martel smiled and picked up a blade himself.

Black smoke filled the shattered remains of the once-proud Fort Grey and rose more than a hundred feet into the air. Many of the surrounding buildings were nothing more than ruins, their reactors detonated by the gargoyle invasion force or farmers trying to take a few of the creatures with them. Not one person was left in the ruined fort. Only gargoyles resided there now.

Small pockets of the remaining humans outside the fort hid in the half dozen houses and shops still standing. From those windows, men and women peered out at large gargoyles as they continued to search the streets. Occasionally, a gargoyle would enter a structure to check it again. If it was alone, the creature would never come out again.

A small group of soldiers had convinced Commander Martel to join them and had managed to escape through a maintenance hatch, after hiding in an auxiliary reactor room until the main attack was over. Communication between the isolated groups had to be done by direct transmission using laser transmitters. One team had mistakenly used a land-line to send a message and was quickly attacked by a dozen gargoyles. They apparently had figured out how to access the computers or one had been left on.

Commander Martel and four other battle-weary troopers holed up in a reserve long-distance transmitter bunker.

Their armour was damaged but still functional. The interior of the structure was a maze of offices, service bays and stored equipment. This made the bunker extremely hard to get into or out of quickly. Buildings where the troopers chose to hide contained a GCR in its own vehicle bay. No one wanted to use them after a civilian used one to try to escape.

He kept broadcasting his status even though no one responded. The troopers knew the gargoyles would soon home in on the transmissions but they did not dare warn him for fear they would be set upon. All they could do was listen.

The brief trip transmissions came over the airwaves:
'I can't stay here any longer. I'm gone!'
<pause>
'I've cleared the buildings. They can't keep up.'
<pause>
'I'm gonna make it!'
<pause>
'Don't worry everyone, I'll send help as soon... assssssssss'

After the attempted breakout, the gargoyles stepped up the building search, finding only the young man's distraught mother. They immediately dragged her into the carcass of the fort and killed her.

Commander Martel looked out one of the communication bunker's windows across to a civilian machine shop where he knew twelve people were hiding. The real object of his observation was the two gargoyles squatting in front of the shop. They both had blade hilts on their newly acquired utility belts, just one of piece of Terran armour they had appropriated.

Because of their wings, the power pack for the suit was removed from the chest pieces, though it did not seem to affect their movements. The frightening thing was, the armour made them look bigger. They did not wear the helmets, gloves or boots because of the major differences in form. The forearm braces were slit down the sides to allow for their scythes.

Martel angled his directional microphone towards the beasts to try to learn their language or at least get a feel for it. His heart almost stopped when he started to pick up their conversation in English and waved at the other troopers near him to listen in.

'... searching all day. They must be all gone now,' said the one on the left in a low, grunting voice.

'We have to be sure before the next gneallarum,' the other gargoyle said.

'In human, Xata, we all have to learn human so we can talk to the slaves.'

'Before the next... it is gneallarum, you know what I say,' it growled in frustration.

'Use that book to get the word.' It said pointing to the text pad on the other's belt.

'Surgery!' it growled happily after a moment of searching.

'No, but close... it is operation. This language is tricky.'

'Anyway, Saturn Fort is next and have a killed line, um, no, deadline. Grrr... I hate this human speech!' It threw the pad into the wall of the communication building.

Martel took the microphone down and turned to the other troopers who waited patiently for whatever orders he would issue. He knew if he ordered an attack they would follow, in spite of the odds of a hundred to one against them.

'We don't know what happened to Major Harte's unit but since those creatures are here we should assume that they did not get through. We will have to warn Fort Saturn ourselves or they'll be wiped out as fast as we were,' he commented before detailing his plans.

The Humans worked diligently for the next half an hour to prepare the building for Martel's plan. Some troopers were not pleased about some of the details, deciding to wait until they were finished before bringing them up.

'Everything is set, sir. I've let the other clusters know of the plan and they're waiting for the signal,' said the acting second in command once the work was finished, 'but I really think you should reconsider the last part of the plan.'

'It's the way it has to be, soldier,' Martel sighed.

'We figured you were going to say that sir, and we've decided to disobey your orders to leave. We're staying for the duration.' The other troopers stepped from behind the computer banks.

'I guess if you disobey that order once then telling you again won't really change things,' Commander Martel smiled. The loyalty shown by these ordinary soldiers was touching and threatened to choke him up, 'Alri... umm... Alright then, we'll have to change the plan for this building.'

*****

CHAPTER IX
Wednesday, 5 April, 2251

The convoy's pace through the forest was steady at best, similar to ploughing a field at the worst. Kain, Chuck and Brian led the way, searching for a path wide enough for the vehicles to pass or even clearing a path where needed. Dolly, Duke and Viper took the left flank, bored but watching for a sneak attack.

TJ, Martin and Dean forced their way through the underbrush on the right flank of the convoy as the vehicles moved easily down the path. Dean and Martin were in the same state as their counterparts on the other side. TJ was in his own world trying to figure out Daniella and Amanda. He was so deep in thought he hardly bothered to scan the trees or even watch where he was going. He stumbled a couple of times over protruding roots, drawing some odd stares from the others.

Sam Cornwall had the only portable beam cannon so she had the honour of being in the middle of the formation, in that location she could step to one side or the other as soon as the fight was on. Daniella was at the rear with Erik and Ann, giving her a good view of TJ. She was still annoyed with herself over what she had said, unaware her feelings for him went as deep or were that difficult to conceal.

In front, Brian called a halt order to the column after the second hour of marching. Two mounds of dirt blocked the path they had been following for the last hour. The mounds were at least six feet tall, thick with mud and debris and had a fallen tree lying across their tops. He had stopped five yards from the structure.

'It doesn't look right guys,' Brian cocked his head to one side.

'You know, I don't like it either,' Kain replied. 'I think I saw a clear path about a mile back.'

'What's up, fellas?' TJ asked, walking up to join them. The stoppage of the convoy had managed to refocus his mind on the current operation.

'Good to see you have your feet again chief,' Kain chuckled. He continued after he received a half-hearted leer from the lieutenant, 'There's a rather large speed bump up ahead.'

'I see,' TJ said peering past them, 'It looks out of place.'

'That's what I said. I think we should back up and go around.'

'You guys are nuts!' Chuck cried as he moved towards the mounds, 'it's just dirt and wood.'

'But it doesn't belong here. Things like that don't naturally form,' TJ shouted. 'Get back here before something bad happens.'

Chuck ignored the three of them, even when Kain started towards him. He walked up to the nearest mound, which was about his height, and put his armoured fist through the dirt. The force of the hit let his arm sink in up to the shoulder joint. He pulled his arm out of the mound and turned to face the convoy.

'It's not that deep. We could blast it away easily,' he shouted.

Kain had been moving up behind him to make sure the trooper did nothing stupid, stopping fifteen feet short of Chuck He stared at Chuck's arm. His forearm was covered in inch-long insects. They had small glowing wings and shimmering mandibles. Images of Old Earth ants scrolled across the identification window of the HUD with a flashing mutation warning. Chuck calmly brushed the little things from his arm. As he did so, the ants being brushed away grabbed onto his hand like it was flypaper. He started to swipe at them more vigorously as he began to panic.

'Take it easy Chuck,' said Kain calmly. He started walking back towards the convoy. Half the troop was now standing on the path, watching the flailing trooper.

'I can't get them off, man!' he shouted. 'Oh shit! They're eating through my suit!'

He had barely got the last bit out when he fell back, into the *ant* hill. The hill collapsed in over him, mercifully concealing the view. Ants swarmed over him, his screams dominated the narrow band communicator. Beneath the painful wailing the troop heard the ants penetrating, shredding him and the suit.

'We should get out of here,' TJ said.

Before he got the troopers more than twenty steps, the ants cut through the fuel lines and punctured Chuck's fission reactor at the same moment. For Chuck, the explosion ended his torture. For the troop, it was lucky his fuel load was low. The explosion incinerated most of the ants, finishing the job Chuck had started. The hill was blasted away almost perfectly, clearing the path.

'Well, at least he cleared the hill,' Brian joked.

'Nice,' Viper said as she smacked him.

Brian and Kain, now the only two point men, carefully picked their way through the debris. They had their blades ready, for what they still did not fully know.

The gap in what looked like a hundred-foot long ant ridge-line was half again as wide as they needed for the vehicles to pass. Nothing was left of Chuck or his armour in the leaves and mix of brown and red dirt. They found his blade in the middle of a cluster of feeding ants eating the crystal that gave the blade its shape.

'Hey, TJ, come and look at this!' Kain hollered.

TJ walked to the remains of the mound and looked closely at the trail of ants, carrying away thin slices of crystal to the largest section of the hill.

'Odd, I've never seen insects that ate or stored crystal.'

'What if, the crystal gives them the energy to make their wings glow and allows their mandibles to cut though armour? Kind of like the way our blades work.'

'That almost sounds like the case, doesn't it? I suppose it's possible; I mean, look at lightning bugs,' Brian added.

'Do you think the crystals have mutated these things at all?' Kain asked.

'Yeah,' TJ said after a pause. 'Well, let's keep moving people. And give these little guys plenty of room.'

Kain signalled the sleds to resume their forward motion. As the convoy moved up to and past the hill, TJ and Dean fell into position on the right flank once again.

They occasionally came upon other equally large anthills. Instead of forcing their way through them, changing directions to avoid them all together achieved the same goal, but slowed their progress and drove them farther west towards the centre of the forest. Sometimes they had to loop around more than a mile to get around a series of mounds and suspicious-looking formations of dirt and wood.

'Hey guys, I'm getting hungry. Do you think we could find a clearing where we could stop for a bite?' Martin asked.

'I suppose we'll have to,' Amanda said, although she was not happy. 'Okay. Kain, Brian, find us a hole in these trees big enough for us to group up. I don't want to sit on this path any longer than we have to.'

The convoy stopped on the path with the foot troopers standing around the vehicles; they scanned the trees around them while the two point men began a search of the area. The search took under ten minutes before the XO of the First Recon and the Second Recon's Blademaster appeared back on the path ahead of the convoy.

'We've got a spot about a quarter mile up ahead. There's a clear path branch that leads straight to it,' Brian told the column.

'Alright! Let's go eat!' Dean replied, seconds before he moved off down the path.

With some smiles and a few laughs, the rest of the group followed him. They soon burst into a beautiful clearing covered in a carpet of brilliant multi-coloured flowers and a few young trees. The contours of the field were reminiscent of a small volcano crater or perhaps an impact crater. Grass covered most of the ground with a few patches of hard red rock.

At first glance the clearing appeared to have a diameter of about two hundred and fifty yards, the circular design making it hard to determine without an actual measurement. Trees ringed the clearing in an almost perfect circle. The lush sea of green, violet and red sloped away from the trees at a gentle angle before rising more steeply to a mound at the centre of the field.

When the rear of the formation finally arrived at the clearing, Dean and the point men were at the top of the hill and the lead vehicle was deep in the valley heading towards the base of the center hill. The left and right flank groups were patrolling around the hill to ensure the area was suitable for them to remain free from threat.

'Hey, there's a dent in this hill,' Dean called.

TJ crested the hill with the rest of the patrol group after his survey was completed, where he was treated to a marvellous view of the ring shaped valley and the indentation at the centre of the hill. Even in the sunlight of the two stars, the depression somehow remained cool.

After a running blade fight and the hungry ants, the group was becoming paranoid and had difficulty settling down. Their world had been turned upside down in less than a week, it had been five days since Commander Martel had been ordered to investigate some *lunatic's* claim of a destroyed convoy. Already nearly a quarter of their fellow militia in the group were dead, not to mention people lost at the base. They had every right to be uneasy, thought TJ.

It was D500 hours before the perimeter check was complete and the entire troop could rest. The GCR and the BRAT were parked at the base of the hill on the north side.

Four troopers ate their lunch next to the hover cars, in case of attack. The remainder of the troops were at the top of the hill, around a small campfire, for visual comfort more for comfort than anything else. They sat around this small source of light with their visors open, discussing what the future might hold and what possible points of origin might these gargoyles have emerged.

The ventilation systems in their suits were working overtime to purify the air. Even so, the air had a stale and stuffy taste to it in spite of the fragrant aroma from the flowers. Some of the younger troopers were having difficulty breathing, their voices were strained while they worked at talking. Coughing punctuated the conversation.

'You know what, I've been thinking...' TJ started.

'Good for you,' Buzz laughed, snapping up the opportunity to get in a shot at his CO. Laughter sprang up from the troops, even TJ but it was the strained laughter people made to relieve stress.

'Old, man, old,' Ann giggled.

'But quick,' Erik chuckled.

'May I continue?' TJ asked when they had calmed down.

'Yeah, sure,' Buzz chuckled, 'go ahead.'

'As I was saying, I think our friends do the same thing as those ants. They eat the crystals that we use as a power-converting instrument; that would explain their wings and those scythes on their arms, and why they're so pissed at us.'

'Okay, we have a mining operation in the Western Crystal fields,' Major Harte said. 'It's very heavily defended. If they're as smart as you say they are, then they must have worked out it would be pointless to attack that installation.'

'They probably saw a BRAT being loaded and followed it. You know those civvies transport drivers are fast and crazy. The gargoyles most likely couldn't catch it even with their speed. Then they must have seen a delivery go to the Miles Research Station and decided to attack the station. All makes some sense now, but where did they come from?' TJ asked.

'That's the real question, isn't it,' Amanda said.

'I do have a theory on that one,' Kain said emerging from his silence. 'It involves the gas planet twenty years ago.'

'Oh... this should be good,' Buzz smiled.

While the conversation at the top of the hill on origins of the gargoyles continued, activity at the base of the mound was more relaxed. Denyse smiled as she playfully fought off the flirtatious advances of the three other troopers with her. Duke was leaning on the GCR next to her, holding her armoured hand casually.

While the gloves did not allow for direct contact, it produced a similar effect. Brian and Martin stood facing her and only occasionally glanced around. Still on duty, Brian looked up, catching movement in the trees.

'There's something up there,' he said, stepping out of the formation.

The smiles faded from the other three as the words sunk in. Duke let go of Denyse and stepped forward to stand next to him.

'Where?'

'There, next to that scraggily-looking tree,' Brian replied pointing up the hill.

'Martin, go tell the others.'

'Yes, sir,' he had already started up the hill at a half-run even as Brian finished his order.

'I'll have a look, Duke. It may be nothing.'

'Oh man, I don't know if we're clear of those things yet. Watch yourself,' said Duke uneasily.

Brian started towards the point where he had seen the movement; Denyse climbed into the GCR gunner chair, powered up the weapon and activated the controls, bringing the turret around to cover Brian with expert precision. By now at full speed to tell the rest of the group what was happening, Martin crested the hill. Out of breath, he took a moment to say anything.

A couple of blades burst to life as the startled troopers sprang to their feet. The energy bolt surprised them even more, catching Martin from behind in his right shoulder with a burst of green light. He was thrown into the middle of their group on the floor of the indentation. Brian saw the bolt erupt from the trees ahead of him and managed to spin around fast enough to see Martin fall into the hill. He whipped around again and saw a totally new creature emerge from the trees. It was clearly reptilian, though any relation to a Terran reptile was not immediately apparent.

'Oh, crap,' he said under his breath.

The reptile had four legs and two arms, looking vaguely humanoid from the front. A long sweeping tail ruined the illusion, as did the cobra-style hood around its head. It had a silver weapon of some sort in its arms resembling a version of a human beam cannon. It swung the barrel of the weapon towards the trooper.

The creature let off a shot of sparkling green at Brian, catching him square in the chest. The shot sent him reeling backwards and on to the ground, crushing the delicate flowers.

The armour took the hit well, enough to allow Brian to roll away to one side and up onto his feet. Once upright again, he slipped on the grass as he began to sprint back to the GCR for cover. A brilliant blue beam creased the sky over his head and impacted the reptile's chest in a blinding shower of white and blue light. When the flash cleared, the injured creature could be seen dragging itself back into the trees.

Brian turned to see it leave and a dozen more come into view. He spun back around to run when three bolts hit him within seconds. The first hit a leg servomotor while the second hit soundly on the shoulder deflector plate, the combined impact was enough to topple the running trooper. On his way down, the third bolt hit the neck joint and went through. Brian hit the ground hard, dug into the dirt and did not get up. Daniella had made it over the lip of the indentation and was in time to see Brian fall. She teetered on the brink of collapse as she saw her XO brought down.

'Brian, no,' she whispered and leaned back. Iceman managed to get beside her before she fell.

TJ came running to them from his place on the edge of the hill's crater, shouting at them, 'Down! Down! Get down!'

Dallas had made it up to look over the hill when TJ ran past him and pushed him back. A split-second later a bolt sailed past where he would have been. Iceman looked at TJ then to the trees where a reptile had fired a bolt at him. He had enough time to turn his back to the shot before it hit him, sending him careening into the red and grey dirt of the crater next to where Martin lay.

TJ saw Iceman fall and lunged at Daniella to knock her down. His outstretched arm took a hit aimed at her and became numb before he grabbed her. They both tumbled into the crater on top of Iceman.

'Get off me, please,' Iceman said, trying to catch his breath.

'Sorry man,' TJ said, 'Stay here with Daniella. Dallas, Viper, come with me. Buzz, take Kain, Dolly and Dean to their right flank.' He shook the arm that had been hit in an effort to wake it up as he ran.

'Sam, go nuts!' Erik yelled from his spotting position beside her on the rim.

The brilliant blue beam seared the air again and again, leaving tracers in the eyes of the troopers and knocking over the reptiles wherever it hit, but they would get up moments later and rejoin the assault. Showers of energy bolts rained down on the vehicles and Duke from the tree line. Duke stood beside the GCR to limit the number of shots coming at him and turn away the bolts making it through, with his blade. Despite his skill, still an odd shot slipped through his twirling blade.

During the flurry of energy bolts, Duke somehow deflected two or three shots to nearly the same spot on the GCR. The consecutive blasting drilled a neat hole in the armour and exposed vital components. A hail of bolts from the reptiles' rifles, forced him to dive behind the GCR. A wild shot hit the hole in the sled and overloaded the internal systems.

'Something's not right here. I have no contacts,' said Denyse from the GCR gunner's seat. 'Wait! Got one, damn... it's beside the BRAT. Duke, look out!'

The turret whirled around and sent a blast of death at the phantom target and instead of a hostile adversary blasted the BRAT. The shot burrowed through the cargo hold at a weakened part of the armour, setting off a series of small explosions amongst the repair and fuel supplies. The combination of beam and blast detonated the main fuel cell in the transport. The force of the explosion blew the GCR onto its side, crushing Duke and at the same time set the vehicle on fire.

Amanda saw the plume of the explosion followed by two columns of smoke and knew what had happened. Her troop was now down to fourteen, including two injured. TJ had taken away seven of her platoon, leaving her with five able-bodied troopers in this dark pit with streaking bolts of green racing overhead. There was no way this could end well, she mused.

That blast was unexpected to say the least, thought TJ. The haze in his mind began to lift. The armour was a great concept, but it had never been designed as a concussion suit. TJ and the two troopers with him had been running past the BRAT when it exploded. The blast knocked all three of them over.

TJ rolled over slowly to avoid further injury but even so he could not move any faster at the moment. He managed to crawl to Viper, who was lying prone and shook her to get her moving again.

The ground was ripped up providing good cover from those lizard creatures for now, but these clumps of red rock would not stand up to any kind of assault.

'Come on, Ashley, let's go! No time for napping,' he said.

'Ouch!' she muttered, putting a hand to her head. 'Let's not do, whatever that was again, okay?'

As she rolled over to get to her feet, TJ crawled to where Dallas lay, giving him a quick push. It was not until he noticed the trooper had not moved or said anything that TJ saw the condition of his armour. The right side he had approached was looking fine. The front side was heavily scored. Damage to the suit ranged from mere scratches to heavy gashes with soot stains and blast marks decorating the suit.

None of the damage to the suit looked as if it could have resulted in injury to its occupant. TJ rolled Dallas on to his back to get a closer look at some of the deeper damage trying to find out why his HUD was showing a dead trooper in front of him. With a heavy thump, Dallas rolled over, exposing his left side and the three-inch round frame rod protruding from the side of the suit, through Dallas' left arm, effectively nailing it to the side of the armour. Dark red blood still oozed around the rod.

'I wish they'd get authorization from me before they install new equipment in my people,' TJ said.

'Damn!' Viper hissed. 'Looks quick, thankfully.'

'Yeah, still ruined his day though. Come on, we have bigger problems,' TJ said getting to his feet.

They ran towards the reptile attack force's left flank occasionally stumbling. Their muscles complained at the exertion. The creatures were advancing on the center hill or were busy dealing with Buzz and the others, not noticing the two of them swing around to attack from the opposite side. Their blades came on in a flash as they drove into the fray.

The closest reptile saw them at the last second, dancing away from Viper in time. Their bodies were nimble for creatures twice the size of TJ. The one next to Viper's target saw her as well, but failed to see TJ, his blade making contact firmly in the creature's breast. Instead of dicing the thing, the attack sent it flying backwards as if it had struck solidly leaving little more than a nasty gash across its chest.

Stunned by the ineffective hit, TJ lowered his guard for a split second before a green bolt blasted him near his left hip.

The shot spun him around, causing him to lose his balance in the process. He finished a complete spin before he landed on his right side aggravating the injuries from the last blast. His assailant had raced up close enough to allow him to bring his blade across the back of the creature's right fore leg, finally getting past the scales, severing it cleanly at the knee. The combination of its speed and the loss of a limb sent the reptile sprawling into a patch of blue flowers.

TJ rolled to his feet, bringing his blade up in time to deflect a bolt into the ground, almost by accident. The shot came from the creature fighting Viper, who promptly kicked the creature to the ground, piercing it through where the heart was presumably located. TJ saw another reptile run up behind Viper and bring its fist down on the back of her helmet. The hit sent her tumbling over the body of its fallen comrade, rolling through the grass for several yards.

'Viper, hang on,' he shouted. His rescue effort was halted by yet another beast not more than three yards away.

TJ assumed the closer you were when these things fired, the more damage was done. His thoughts were based on the fact that his side was killing him and Iceman was mostly functional after he was hit. If he could not stop it, the next shot was going to hurt a lot – that pleasant thought one he did not need at the moment.

The beast in front of him was as tall as he was in his armour. The look in its golden eyes told TJ the dragon-thing was about to fire, clearly discussing options was out of the question. Its determination was blasted away by a sapphire blue beam from the hill causing its body to be thrown forward onto TJ's blade. Both flew three yards before skidding across the grass to a stop with TJ pinned under the dead green reptile, looking up at two more of the creatures with what he presumed were unhappy looks on their faces. Unable to remove his blade, he closed his eyes, waiting for the darkness.

*****

CHAPTER X
Wednesday, 5 April, 2251

Martel closed his eyes and thought a moment, then ordered, 'Send the signal to the clusters.'

'Yes, sir!' said the young woman sitting at the radio. 'Go... All clusters go!'

With that simple phrase, the vehicle doors on half of the remaining buildings rolled open and eight GCRs burst forth along with four BRATs. The gargoyles heard or sensed the signal and began to converge on the point of origin, racing towards the speeding vehicles as soon as they saw the humans running. More than fifty gargoyles swept past Martel's building and another ten emerged from the field in front of the sleds. All of the gargoyles now had some manner of armour protection that did not seem to slow them down.

Martel and his small group waited quietly as the sleds continued to transmit their status of escape until the message was received they were less than one hundred feet from the lead gargoyle and within one hundred yards of the blockade group in the field.

Everything was proceeding as planned.

'Now, private, begin transmission to the auxiliary broadcast tower... full power,' Martel said. There was a hint of amusement in his manner since he was turning the enemy advantage against them. His situation was no better than the one his people were in out there in the field, and he was inviting his certain death with this transmission.

The convoy stopped transmission a second before a powerful signal spread out from the tower, hitting the creatures with such force some of the flying monsters crashed to the ground. Some managed to stay in the air with considerable effort. The instant the swarm recovered they turned and raced back to the shadow of the buildings of the once-mighty Fort Grey.

As the gargoyles reached point-blank range on their return to the fort, gunners in the sleds blasted the entire group. A shower of matter pelted the vehicles, obscuring the windshields and covered the thick grass with a new coating of green colouring.

Seeming to ignore the carnage behind them, the main body of the gargoyle force from the field converged on the reserve transmitter, with even more closing from the fort. The doors and windows burst as they forced their way inside. Twenty or more gargoyles searched the building, crashing noisily through some strategically placed barricades, stepping over or around several conspicuous yellow and red trunks.

The barricade at the east end of the last room of the building failed, exposing the occupants to the gargoyles. Green eyes flared at the sight of three humans standing next to a GCR in the center of the room, in the middle of the building.

'Human,' grunted a large gargoyle, 'put down your weapons and surrender to the Bregan.' The gnashing of its teeth and tusks while it spoke almost drowned out the words.

'Bregan? That's what you call yourselves?' Martel asked, stunned he was actually conversing with one of the animals. He stepped forward, keeping the attention of the creatures.

'That is correct, small creature. You will surrender now.' The animal was huge even with the several yards between them.

'I really think you've overestimated your chances here, friend.' He edged his troops into the sled, at the same time pointing to the red cable secured to the rear.

'Friend?' the Bregan asked.

It stared at the cable leading to the back of the room and into a large stack of the yellow and red trunks. It turned to look the other way at a long hallway that had been created leading to the vehicle bay doors, its eyes jumping from each newly recognised trunk. What was going to happen became obvious to the creature when the GCR door slammed shut. It jumped in front of the sled and was sent crashing into a computer by the blue beam emitted by the turret.

'Punch it, corporal,' Commander Martel said firmly. 'We'll be gone, folks,' he added.

The GCR shot past the fallen Bregan and its compatriots before flying down the freshly constructed hall. The cable between the sled and the detonation lever pulled taut as the GCR cleared the building, detonating a small explosion to detach the cable from the lever after activation. The separation explosion started a chain reaction beginning in the launch room where the sled had been parked. Before the shockwave of the initial explosion reached the walls of the room, a wave of explosions commenced at the back of the building and vaporized the entire compound of small buildings behind the rocketing gopher. The shock wave tossed the tiny vehicle around like a surfer on a tidal wave.

The remains of Fort Grey could not withstand the blast from these surrounding buildings, collapsing in on itself and whatever residents remained inside. The entire complex of buildings was wiped from the map. Secondary explosions lit the early evening sky, visible even beyond the usual half mile. The GCR carrying Commander Martel joined the rest of the vehicles moments later, and together they raced north-westerly, towards Port Mars, and the capital of the Eden peninsula.

*****

'Play the message back,' Major Harte ordered.

'Uh, yes ma'am,' Martin stuttered.

The strong transmission had interrupted her thoughts as to her next move. She ordered Iceman to try to raise Fort Grey, the originator of the signal. Martin replayed the transmission for Amanda.

'This is Commander Martel of Fort Grey.
Gargoyle-like creatures, calling themselves Bregan, have overrun our installation. Eighty percent of my staff and civilian personnel are dead or captured. The survivors and I are on route to Port Mars to sound the general alarm if it has not already been done.
The gargoyles intend to destroy Fort Saturn next as far as I have been able to determine. I fear for my people that are on their way there. Good luck to all humanity and may Sol forever shine on you.'

'Grey is gone? No way, man... no way!' Martin exclaimed.

'Believe it,' Johnny interrupted. 'I'm not even getting static.'

A primal howl shattered the relative peace at the top of the hill, indicating the Bregan had arrived in the clearing. The cry came from the trees opposite the reptiles and was getting closer. 'Wow,' Ann said with understated emotion. 'This day sucks!'

The remaining soldiers with Amanda snapped on their blades in anticipation of a rear attack. Sam spun from battling the reptiles to provide cover for Amanda and her squad. They did not have to wait long before their antagonists rose over the crest of the hill.

These Bregan seemed different from those that had attacked the group earlier. They were wary, not rushing in on the humans.

Their dark red-brown skin was almost completely hidden by the patches of armour they wore and each carried a blade in addition to their own scythes.

'So that's what the survivor meant,' Amanda whispered.

'What?' Ann asked.

'Nothing, never mind. Advance, people. Make them think.'

The six slowly moved forward in a hexagon formation to provide the best cover for one another. Watching the humans approach, the Bregan stood with their blades drawn. They were preparing to leap into battle when the brilliant blue lightning bolt from Sam's beam cannon hit the creature on the far right of the dozen. The armour it was wearing took most of the damage before the fatal shot could reach the creature within. The force of the shot hurtled the Bregan backwards off the hill.

The eleven remaining Bregan took that as a sign to engage. Four soared high into the air while the rest surged across the ground. Their eyes burned fiercely, green flames trailing behind as the creatures raced forward. The squad's thoughts... this was going to be a slaughter.

The reptile standing over the fallen Viper almost broke its neck when it twisted to see where the howl had come from. Reptiles throughout the crater ceased their conflict with the humans to stare after the howl. TJ, Viper and the three remaining troopers on the other side of the battleground stared at the beasts that moments previously were making short work of them. TJ, taking advantage of the break in fighting, squirmed out from under the dead reptile and crawled under the reptiles' field of vision towards Viper.

'What's happening?' Viper asked in a hoarse whisper.

'The gargoyles are here. They must have followed us,' TJ whispered in return.

As if on cue, four gargoyles emerged in the air above the hill. The reptiles raced off to the hill and the gargoyles with frightening speed. The creatures tore up the ground in their frenzied haste to retreat, pieces of grass and flowers flying into the air. Humans in the valley pursued them but were slowed by their numerous wounds and their battered armour.

'I think they know each other, guys,' TJ commented, a half-hearted grin on his face.

The approaching massive Bregan forms slowly surrounded the six humans while two of the airborne creatures landed behind the group, completing the circle. The last two Bregan in flight streaked towards Sam and her cannon. She fired a chilling blue beam of death at the lead Bregan with impeccable aim. The Bregan recognized the incoming shot for what it was and what it could do if it reached its target and readied its blade. It brought the blade, left to right, across its chest and almost perfectly deflected the beam away from itself.

The deflected shot had unplanned consequences, hitting the second creature. The beam had amazingly found its way through a gap in the side of the armour plating the Bregan was wearing. The sack of mushy flesh and armour plate hit the ground with a hollow sound, dead.

'Thank our lucky stars, it's not good at that.' Sam dropped her cannon and swung her blade off her hip. She triggered the shards to form the blade and prepared herself for an electric sabre dance.

Even though Sam was ready for the fight, events occurred around her that prevented her from engaging. Seconds before her adversary landed and was in blade range, an energy bolt streaked past her head and struck the Bregan in its left wing. Two more shots tore through the air impacting into the Bregan's chest and propelling it backward into the legs of one of the Bregan circling the six humans. From that point forward, the tide of battle changed. It was obvious even the Bregan had sensed the change, but they fought on.

Both humans and Bregan alike looked up at Sam, who was the only visible being in that direction. She in turn, was looking over the edge of the hill at her saviours. Although it felt like an eternity, it was only several seconds before the reptiles burst over the hill with a deafening hiss from them or the scales of their armour.

The Bregan were seemingly taken aback for a moment at the sight of the creatures. Then, slowly, a low grumbling roar began to emanate from the Bregan as they turned towards the reptiles. With the Bregan distracted and the humans apparently forgotten, the beleaguered squad took the opportunity to cut down two of the armoured Bregan before they flashed back into reality.

TJ and his group of mostly wounded, mounted the hill and stood beside the stunned heavy weapons specialist in time to watch the fray. The thought of engaging with the rest of the troop entered his mind but he held his people back and watched.

The fight was essentially one-sided slaughter and would be quickly over. The Bregan engaged each human in sword play until inevitably a reptile shot it in the back from a safe distance. If turned to fight the reptile enemy, the human's blade would cut it down. Several Bregan fell that way although three of them continued to put up a good fight. They fought as a group and managed to take down Martin who moved in too close to aid the already injured Iceman, before they were stopped. Two reptiles fell during the fray before the end came as a result of a last ditch charge by the Bregan.

TJ and his people cautiously approached the gathering of humans and reptiles as the last gargoyle settled to the ground. The two sides were eyeing each another nervously. The reptile force was not as confident as when they first appeared now that they were outnumbered in a confined location with the troopers. Dolly went to Iceman's side to tend to his wounds heedless of the creatures looming over him.

'So now what?' Daniella asked of no one in particular. She never once took her eyes from the six-foot tall creatures standing close to her.

'Amanda, do we keep fighting?' Ann asked.

'Not sure, Ann, but it looks like we won't have to.'

'...they talk a lot, Kraston,' said one of the reptiles.

'Hey! I thought that would be our line,' Buzz chuckled.

'You fight the Bregan, human.' The largest creature calling itself Kraston addressed his reply to Amanda.

'Yes, we do. We didn't want to but they left us no choice.'

'They do start things,' a younger-looking reptile said.

'This is no place to talk. Will you come with us to our city in the trees? There we can provide answers to each other and tend to our wounded,' Kraston offered.

'We don't really have a choice here, do we?' TJ asked, looking at the seven deadly creatures ahead of him.

'No, you do not.'

'Well, then we agree. Give us a moment to deal with our dead and gather our equipment,' Amanda said as diplomatically as possible. She did not enjoy the idea of being captured, whether in action or by word play alone.

*****

CHAPTER XI
Wednesday, 5 April, 2251

Commander Martel's convoy had made reasonable progress through the fields of peacefully waving long-grass and into the Brossan Hills in the hours after their escape. No sign of pursuit by the Bregan could be detected but that gave little comfort to the men and women crammed into the twelve vehicles. Shock still held its grip on the survivors of Fort Grey, there was little chatter.

'Stop up ahead private Aceves,' Martel said to the pilot of his GCR.

'Yes sir. We are exposed up on this ridgeline,' he said as the sled came to a stop.

'Agreed, however we need to see what we got away with. Corporal Dalar, get the GCRs to form a perimeter around the BRATs so we can start an inventory.'

'Yes sir,' the corporal popped the rear hatch and began waving and calling orders to the other hovercraft to setup the compound.

Martel was the next out and surveyed the vehicles and troopers as they moved around. His earlier worries about losing a handful of troopers to a mission gone wrong now seemed almost comical. His base was levelled and as best he could figure these few men and women were all that remained of his command. He thought he would have felt more in this situation.

'Sir, we've got the camp set and I've ordered one trooper to go through each vehicle to get a list of anything not part of the vehicles,' Corporal Dalar said once the orders were finished.

'Good, well done corporal,' Martel put a hand on the young man's shoulder. 'Assemble the rest of the group in front of the transports. We may as well take inventory of the people too.'

A few minutes later a group of armoured people stood in loose formation in front of Commander Martel. Including the twelve troopers inside the vehicles the count was down to thirty-two. Thirty-two from over five hundred. That was when it started to sink in for Martel.

'Well here we are then, the last of Fort Grey. We do not know where Major Harte's group are or if they've managed to get to Fort Saturn. In light of this morning's attack my gut says they hadn't made it in time.' He paused for a moment to steel himself, 'Port Mars is a much larger city than the Grey was or even what Saturn hopefully still is. It is also a military facility. Their weaponry is much stronger than ours, their defences more solid. If mankind it going to make it clear of this latest mess then that is where our stand will be. Our group, our thirty-two, must be the ones to raise the alarm. We must succeed where others have failed. With any luck we will be able to return to pay tribute to those that have given us this opportunity.'

The group applauded his impromptu speech and quickly began talking with each other about their ordeals during the escape. As the troopers taking inventory returned they were told of the speech and what it would mean for the group. Some did not participate in the chatter, opting instead to stand alone and stare at the gently swaying grass or out into the hazy horizon. Martel knew it would not be long before they all started contemplating the future, likely the end of mankind.

'Sir, inventory from the sleds,' Captain Ladore handed a touch pad to the commander. Martel was pleased to see she had made it out of the fort's destruction.

'Thank you, Captain.' Martel looked down the flickering blue list that should have been much longer. Two of the BRATs were civilian transports, not much there but a first-aid kit. He noticed the most disturbing fact that all the vehicles were noticeably low on fuel. 'To die because we're running out of fuel is not acceptable. Captain, take the fuel from the two civilian transports and distribute it between the GCRs. I want them as full as you can make them.'

'Yes, sir,' she saluted and began barking orders. All fuel and equipment were to be transferred to the rest of the convoy. 'Sir? Should we detonate the derelicts?'

'Negative. If those things want to make a nest out of these BRATs and make some brats of their own then let them have it.'

Martel was pleased to have an activity to keep the troopers occupied even if it was mind-numbing equipment transfer. He knew he could make it to Port Mars if he could work out the fuel. He simply had to; with all those people lost, how many more would fall?

'Sir, we've completed the transfer and we're at sixty percent in the GCRs and forty percent in the BRATs,' Captain Ladore said after several minutes running the numbers. 'Calculations are showing we might make it to New Terra but not much further.'

'Damn,' Commander Martel looked to the sky for some guidance but all he found was Bane looking back at him.

'Commander, I've been looking over our charts and we're pretty close to where Lieutenant Marso's squad found that convoy,' Private Iody said from a small cluster of troopers.

'Interesting, they reported a large debris field. I wonder if there may be items lingering despite the destruction?' Martel thought out loud.

'Sir, if I remember correctly from TJ's report, the wrecks were blown to bits except for the cargo section of one of the BRATs. There won't be much left, especially if that one was looted afterward,' Captain Ladore said.

'That may be true, Captain but not all vehicles of the original search and rescue dispatch were located before the Second Recon was attacked. I think it's reasonable to expect more vehicles to be in the area. Assemble a squad to salvage the possible wrecks.'

'Yes, sir,' she shook her head in a quick flash as she turned to the gathered troopers. 'Listen up! You twelve here.' She waved to the four groups of three that had formed. 'Come with me for salvage duty. The rest of you go through the sleds to ensure they are ready to move once we get back.'

'Yes, ma'am,' they saluted.

'Stay alert, Captain. The Bregan have jumped our squads twice in these hills. It's possible they are still waiting.'

'Understood, Commander,' she replied, saluting.

The commander stood solemnly as he watched the squad leave. The troopers behind him milled about behind him, completing the work assigned but without hurry. He did not like watching the departing squads normally but he felt he had to this time.

Captain Ladore wanted to get this walk over with in a hurry. She felt it was a waste of resources and an unnecessary delay in the evacuation plan. Too many people had died just doing their job they did not need to risk their lives on these secondary jaunts. Her need to expedite the journey got them to the wreckage of the remaining BRAT in just over an hour.

'Okay, boys and girls, have a look around for useful items, if there are any. Private Palson, have a look over the north ridge, Smith over the west. TJ came in from the south and we came in from the east so that should cover it.'

'Yes, ma'am.' They saluted and moved off.

The ten troopers remaining in the valley rummaged through the debris. Three troopers went through the remainder of the BRAT with a not dissimilar lack of enthusiasm to the troops back at camp. Those outside the wreck meandered amongst the various bits of metal, kicking the odd piece here or there. Captain Ladore watched the uninspired salvaged from the east ridge and shook her head again, what a waste.

Half an hour into the search, the troops in the valley began to return to Ladore's position with little more than a couple handfuls of crystals and a first-aid kit. The only thing Private Smith had when he returned from the west side was a shrug. Ladore threw her hands into the air in frustration at this useless exercise. She looked to the north for Palson to return so they could return to the convoy and be on their way to Port Mars.

Ten minutes passed as the last of the squad formed up before Captain Ladore gave in to curiosity and signalled the troopers to follow. She made her way over to the north ridge to see what happened to the Private she had sent out. The far side of hill showed no signs of the boy or his vehicle.

'Should we send a call out for him Captain?' Corporal Canden asked, in an unnecessary whisper.

'As much as I don't think we have anything to worry about we should probably keep our communication to short range,'

They moved further north looking for any signs of human passage. Several minutes passed before Corporal Opedey called out to the group on a tight short ranged frequency. They paused for a moment to listen for the tell-tale screech of Bregan but it never came. With no sign of an impending attack, the squad gathered with the Corporal on the eastern edge of the zone where Palson would have come.

'Report Corporal,' Ladore said as she walked up.

'I've got some tracks heading north, Captain. Both armoured foot traffic and a vehicle skid mark heading further north. Looks like a GCR sized vehicle.'

'Great, then he isn't lost just doing his job. Let's go then. Keep eyes on the horizon folks. It's getting dark soon so we'll be able to spot any Bregan pretty easy if they're moving around with those wings,' she waved to the squad to start moving north. 'The sooner we find him the sooner we can get back to actually escaping from these stupid animals.'

The squad moved forward through the haze with nothing more to track than a line of rusty-beige line through the gently waving long grass of the hills. Spots of crushed grass were the only indication a trooper had walked ahead of them over the hills.

They crested the next green hill at a fast walking pace with the promise of a return trip and the faint hope of safety growing. The valley beyond quietly stole each when it revealed itself as a deep cut in the landscape filled with trees with gently rustling blue leaves. The whispered hiss only infuriated the troopers.

'Those things must be twenty feet tall in a twenty foot valley. We're not going to be able to see anything!' Corporal Deves flapped an arm in the direction of the trees as if to shoo it away.

'It's like the ground is flat coming off the top of this hill and on to the next. Did they design it that way? Because it's kinda cool.' Private Smith stepped up to soak in the view.

'There weren't any trees when Brossan made these hills. Tell you what, you stay up here and smile at your trees while the rest of us look for Mr. Palson,' Captain Ladore said.

Smith was happy enough to stay up on the rise as a lookout while the others followed the vehicle and trooper tracks into the valley. They entered the trees where something large had ploughed into the tree line leaving a massive hole. The path of destruction was extensive, large enough to suggest the disabled vehicle was a BRAT. Even a BRAT was going to be messed up if it drove into this many good sized trees.

'Opedey, Nemdeneu, clear the path. Hoss, Pitsey and Canden take the left. You four take the right. Stay sharp,' Ladore ordered before taking position at the rear of the formation with Deves. They were not going to get much warning if those things were waiting and she did not want to be the first to greet them.

The two troopers at the front had started out with at least a moderate amount of energy but now lazily hacked at the ruined vegetation that was already cut down at a ten degree angle to the right. Troopers to both sides watched with increasing tension as the foliage and undergrowth intensified and cut visibility to less than twenty-five feet. A hundred yards into the little forest the angle of the slice into the woods ended only to be replaced by a massive gouge into the ground churning up the taupe coloured soil. Forty feet further on was the mangled and upside down wreck of a BRAT. The glass of the cockpit was smashed and the roof was caved in. They would have to find another entry point.

'Captain!' A voice from the wreck called, 'Thank the light you're here. Those creatures are snooping around and more than a couple. I couldn't get out.'

'Palson? Get out here,' Ladore moved to the side of the wreck. 'Secure me a perimeter,' she shouted to the rest of the squad.

The troopers fanned out around the wreck while Private Palson joined Ladore at the left side hatch. He looked around expecting to be attacked at any moment.

'Report!' She was not too concerned about an attack with the whole squad around.

'I followed some tracks to the BRAT and went inside to check on supplies. I had just finished an initial inventory when I started hearing some scratching on the plating. At first I thought it was the rest of the squad but when I heard some grunts and growls. I stayed low until I heard boot steps up the cut and that's when I called out.'

'When did the growling stop?'

'Only about ten minutes ago, according to my HUD.'

'You may have wanted to start by mentioning that point, private.' She turned to the nearest group of troopers and called out, 'Eyes up! We have hostiles in the immediate area.'

'My take on the supplies is limited, Captain. We should be able to load everything into a couple totes, which also happen to be inside. We just need to dump some personal items first.'

'Great. Opedey and Canden, go with Palson into the wreck and gather our goods. We need to be finished with this nonsense scavenger hunt now!'

The three troopers had been gone several minutes before a group of heavily muscled Bregan descended from the canopy. Their glowing green spans lit the darkening woods. The rapid drop counteracted the easy targets the auras made of them. While the troopers were ready for a fight the direction of the attack was unanticipated.

Corporal Hoss died before the Bregan had even set foot on the ground. A clean swipe by a forearm scythe split the trooper's helmet and wedged the armoured body around the creature's arm. Private Nemdeneu reacted, diving at the pinned attacker and pierced it through the chest. While the creature died, Nemdeneu stood and fatally smiled at his handiwork. When the shards of a blade sprouted from his own chest, he continued to smile at the irony and collapsed on top of the growing pile of bodies.

Captain Ladore took her turn at the grizzly disassembly line and buried her blade into Nemdeneu's killer's side. 'Regroup!' she called even before looking around.

The falling body of the Bregan attacker brushing past her was the only warning she had of another attack. The corpse still had a glow on its eyes as it fell but that was likely due to the blade that had been thrust between its wings and was now spewing crystal shards out its forehead.

'Thank you private.' She did not care what her name was, 'grab your weapon and we'll get Palson and his group out here!'

'Yes ma'am,' the trooper grabbed the hilt, hit the switch to deactivate the blade and jumped into the BRAT.

Ladore reached down once the trooper had left and picked up her own weapon also choosing to deactivate the shimmering blade rather than trying to pull it out. A quick reconnoitre told her no further danger existed for the squad after a pair of troopers finished off the last visible Bregan at the front of the overturned vehicle. Their killing blows were excessive but they could vent all they wanted. They had to get out of here and a couple extra swings would not slow them.

She turned back to the opening on the side of the BRAT a moment later, waiting for the troopers inside to return. Calling out was not an option, no matter how badly they needed to get going. The Bregan could hear or sense long range communication and who knew if short range was a factor. With likely more of them in the area, there was no sense broadcasting their location.

'Come on, come on,' she muttered. She looked up and down the side of the wreck.

Troopers converged as she waited and each relayed their armour status as they arrived. The likelihood of good news lessened with each report. Fuel reserves were starting to show signs of severe depletion and the crystals in the blades were weakening. Where in the dark were those idiots? She gave up even though it had only been five minutes since they went in. She began waving troopers closer to start a sweep of the vehicle. Maybe Palson and the group ran into another creature in the massive inverted hovercraft.

'Captain!' Palson called out loudly as he exited finally. 'We got the supplies.'

'By the light! Sol forget you for yelling like that!' Deves waved a dismissive hand.

'What?'

'Forget it, let's move. We're getting out of here,' Ladore started to walk off.

'Captain, there's still a crate inside.'

'Leave it. I'm not wasting any more time here. Tell me what we do have but do it while we walk!'

Private Palson detailed the one crate and four quick packs of crystals totalling thirty-six individual shards. One box of eight unpowered blade hilts and two charges of reactor fuel for the power armour finished off his list. The squad had fully cleared the wreck by the time he had realized they were moving.

'There's two full power cells back there,' he started to go back, 'two people each and we'll be in great shape!'

'That's far enough, Private.' Captain Ladore spun around. 'We no longer have the luxury of picking up every scrap. Let's just take what we have and get back to the convoy.'

'Does that include our wounded?' Deves asked.

'Those two weren't wounded, they're dead. We can't afford to slow down for any reason. Let's go!'

'That's cold Captain,' Opedey said.

Ladore said nothing but instead stared at their faces for a moment then turned and proceeded down the cut. The troopers were slow to follow but fell into step reluctantly. The captain felt bad about leaving the bodies but if they were any slower moving out, there would be thirteen bodies instead of two and she did not want to die out here. The squad moved through and out of the trees in silence with the troopers keeping a watchful eye on the diminishing canopy and undergrowth but keeping a noticeable gap from the Captain. She had not noticed since she was charging up the hill, not turning around for anything.

Upon reaching the top of the hill she finally stopped and looked around. Private Smith was not standing on the ridge admiring his magical blue trees as she thought he would be; in fact he was nowhere to be seen. She dialled up her suit's image enhancer to get a clearer look at everything within a half mile range. Nothing.

'Where's Smith?' the young private that had saved her life back at the BRAT asked.

'Gone, he's gone. Let's keep moving people. It's dark and we still have a long haul,' Ladore waved them on.

'Wait... what?' Palson stepped up, 'We're going to leave him?'

'That's correct, Private. We're not going to commit any more resources to this pointless exercise. Especially for some romantic fool who can't see past a few trees.'

'That's unacceptable, Captain! Those things attacked us in there so they probably got him out here. He may be hurt and...'

'If they attacked then he's dead.'

'Commander Martel wouldn't...'

'The Commander will agree with me. We survived because the whole squad was down there. He was alone. Maybe one on one he could win out but alone against many he had no chance.'

Palson was livid. He stomped around the hill waving his arms and apparently screaming inside his helmet although no sound came from his suit. He had hit the kill switch for his external speakers before he started his tirade. The troopers around him shuffled uncomfortably while they watched, backing away. Captain Ladore was still furious at the insubordination but struggled not to react to the display. After a couple minutes, Opedey grabbed Palson and used hand signals to tell him to turn on his communication system. Ladore found a new love for those kill switches, while it was possible to shout out if the suit lost power the kill switch actively blocked communication both into and out of the suit.

'Now that Mister Palson is done with his pantomime, we're moving out,' she said.

'But Captain, Smith is...'

'Enough, Private. We're leaving now. If you want to stay and look then consider yourself relieved of duty,' Ladore said. She turned and marched back towards the convoy.

After brief indecision, the squad fell in line. Palson was the last to join the procession. He continually looked back to the hill overlooking the blue trees in the hope the missing trooper would reappear.

*****

The creature called Kraston led the tattered and damaged remains of the First and Second Recon squads through the denser part of the trees in a westerly direction. The humans managed to keep an eye on the reptiles walking beside and behind, even at a distance of up to thirty feet. This ability to watch their watchers was due to clever terraforming, which provided undergrowth development limited to three feet in height. It meant they could not simply cut and run without their captors tracking them down quickly.

TJ watched the head creature move and admired the strength of the armour-quality scales he wore as an integrated part of his skin. The scales glittered gold and, despite the heavy action he had been engaged in, did not seem to hold any dirt. TJ imagined if you were to listen closely enough you could hear a metallic scraping of his skin.

Kraston walked tall and proud, not once turning to keep a watchful eye on his escort. His four legs made little noise as he gracefully moved through the foliage of the forest. The large cobra-like hood on his head gently pushed through the low hanging branches with a slight turn of the head, so they would not bother him.

Buzz and Dolly were carrying between them a makeshift gurney constructed of vehicle parts. Iceman lay motionless on the stretcher, a nasty-looking gash across his abdomen and down to his right knee. He had a medium sized dent on the left side of his helmet, where something had probably hit causing his unconsciousness. The blow kept the normally mouthy heavy weapons specialist quiet.

'Kraston, where are we going?' TJ asked, running to catch up with the golden reptile.

'To my city near the edge of the forest.'

'May I ask how did your kind learn to speak our language so well?'

'Answers will come in time, human. Be patient,' said a shimmering brown reptile that had crept up on him. TJ noticed it kept its rifle at the precise angle to put him back with Johnny if he got out of line.

'Oh right; sorry,' he replied, carefully stepping back in formation next to Buzz. He looked back at the unconscious trooper before saying anything. 'The entire species is like a swarm of Majors, no doubt,' he added seriously. Buzz grinned.

'Just don't do a lot of talking, chief, and we'll be okay.'

Most of TJ's squad laughed at his humour, drawing quizzical looks from the other squad and a few of the reptiles.

'You just be quiet mister, or I'll take your armour away.' More soft laughs from the humans caused some reptiles to shake their heads.

They walked for the remainder of the day, making camp under the massive canopy of the trees. The humans erected a tarp for their camp. It was large enough to provide cover for themselves and the equipment they managed to salvage from the battleground. The reptiles moved off into the trees and made their camp from some supplies that seemed to have been buried or set aside near the largest of the immediate tree cover. They used their tails and lower limbs to clear the ground before they set up. The creatures were finished setting camp much faster than their human companions, taking the opportunity to eat while they studied their fellow travellers. In the human camp, Dolly and Sam were looking after Johnny, who was still unconscious, while the three senior officers conferred around a small cook fire.

'Anyone ever hear the expression, 'Out of the frying pan and into the fire'? It's not quite that bad yet, but it doesn't look good,' TJ murmured.

'I see what you mean, TJ,' Amanda said in an equally hushed voice, 'I need ideas from you two.'

Daniella stated, 'The two options are obvious. We can either fight them before we get to wherever they're taking us, or we sit and see what happens.'

'Anything else we can do? I'm not overly fond of either of those courses of action,' Amanda said scanning the reptile's camp.

'There is one more option, we could run. However, the way those things move, I'd bet real money we couldn't make it a mile, especially with Johnny in the state he's in,' TJ said.

'You're right, TJ. We can't fight or run in the condition we all are in,' Amanda said after a short pause. 'Okay then, for now we'll sit tight and get what R & R we can.'

'Rest and Repair?' Daniella asked with a half-smile for her friend.

'Yeah, smart ass. Let's start with fixing up Johnny's armour, then the rest,' Amanda ordered.

'Already on it, chief,' Daniella replied as she turned away.

'TJ, get a couple of your people to go through the salvage and collect all the extra weapons and armour plates. I want an inventory list in two hours.'

'Yes, ma'am,' TJ replied, 'and, Amanda. I'm sorry for the grief I've caused you this last week or so. You've really got it together now.' With that he turned and walked off towards the rest of the camp.

Amanda was caught completely off guard by his comment and could only stare after her long-standing, self-proclaimed enemy. Lately her view of him had been warming, but she was not sure it could be called liking yet. She had no idea if this was a tricky prelude to another of his pranks or if he actually meant it. After a minute or so, she stood up and walked back to the group. She decided she would keep an eye on Mr. TJ Marso.

The eyes of the five troopers sitting next to Johnny's cot shifted to TJ as he stepped into the firelight a few moments later. He stood in the ring of his squad members and silently surveyed them. Through the visors of the troopers' armour, he could see a mix of determination, fear and weariness.

These six people had survived events that, until recently, were a thing of movies and books – certainly not even in the fine print of what they signed up for. They were the only remaining members of his command. The people on the Eden peninsula were tough but these troopers were the cream of the crop. TJ respected each of them more than he would ever let on. By now, everyone knew the Bregan had destroyed Fort Grey and that Commander Martel and some of the others had survived. Where they were right now was anyone's guess, hopefully safely on their way to Port Mars.

'Okay, boys and girls, listen up, it looks like we're going to let these reptiles make the first move so we have to be productive in the meantime.'

'What's the order, chief?' Buzz asked.

'We're going to do a rotation shift, three up and three asleep. While we are up, we will be repairing and scrubbing our armour. Remember to keep the circuits and gears clean. One of the three up will be checking fuel and power levels. Try to keep us all at full.'

'Gotcha, boss. Who's on the first shift?'

'Ken, Ashley and I will take first shift. Ken, you know best what Johnny's condition is, so you take care of him. Ash, you start the fuelling operation and I'll start some armour repair.'

'Yes, sir!'

They moved to their roles of sleeping or working.

Viper started by checking Johnny's power stats as Dolly tended to his medical needs. TJ went to the salvage and began to sort it into three piles. First was an armour pile where he placed the undamaged pieces that had been removed from both the dead humans and the fallen Bregan. It had been a morbid job but it was a necessary step in survival for the rest of them.

Next, he divided the wrecked weapons from the power and fuel sources as a safety precaution and to provide material for the power supply stockpile. Occasionally Viper would stop by to pick up a power cell or retrieve some fuel to apply to the recharge of one suit or another. She never said much but her weariness visibly showed in her slower motions. At one point, Dolly came by and lifted Dean's old armour torso plating to put it on Johnny.

'He doesn't look good, TJ,' he said picking up another plate of armour, examining it before throwing it away.

'Will he make it to Fort Saturn?' TJ asked without looking up from the task at hand.

'He should. Daniella and Sam are helping me with him right now, but no one here is an actual medic.'

'What about our reptilian friends? Would they help out?' TJ lifted his head to look in their direction.

'Them? I don't trust them yet.'

'Okay, but we may need their help. Keep it open,' he said tapping his helmet.

'Yes, sir.' He walked away with his armour prize.

Amanda stood next to Ann in almost absolute darkness outside the range of light of the small fire, staring at the other camp. There was not a lot of movement, but the light from their fire glinted off the impossibly shiny scales. She was not sure if they were natural for them or some type of armour. 'How's it look, Ann?' Amanda asked in a whisper.

'Maybe four in the camp and two in the forest somewhere. That leader thing sent one ahead to their city, no doubt.'

'Do you think you can do it?'

'I'll need help, probably Kain. He seems to know his way around a blade.'

'Okay,' Amanda consented, 'Get him and do it.'

'TJ won't be happy,' Ann pointed out.

'Let me worry about TJ. You just get us out of this situation.' She stole a quick glance to TJ and the tasks his group had started working on. 'Yes, Ma'am.' She walked off.

TJ paused in his task to stand and stretch as much as the armour allowed. He had been carefully sorting for two hours and was tired. He picked up four of the blades he had found in the salvage and walked over to where Ken and Ashley were working.

'I have an idea on how to use these blades to our advantage.'

Glancing over Johnny's sleeping form to the weapons, Ken saw they were badly mangled and looked useless.

'As what, paper weights?' he grinned. Viper smiled with him.

'No, well... maybe,' TJ examined them again. 'No, I was thinking that since these four are only missing their power source, we could modify them and install them into the forearm armour'

Intrigued, Viper stopped what she was doing, 'How do you mean, TJ? Blades hard-wired into a suit?'

'Sort of... I was watching those creatures.' He twirled a finger in the air for a moment then snapped, 'Bregan, and how they go in a fight. They primarily use their scythes as a defensives tool and now rely on the blades they took as their offensives weapon. They lasted longer against two enemies than we do against one.'

'I'm sorry, so what are we doing again?' Dolly asked.

'We're going to make ourselves some scythes or at least some forearm defensives fields'

TJ knelt down and began to scratch out his idea for an arm shield on a scrap armour plate with a laser torch. It took several minutes to get the details to work out, but it looked good. TJ was going to get the second shift to start preparing these shields. He sent Viper to wake the sleeping troopers.

She returned shortly with Buzz, Erik and Amanda, not the troopers he was expecting, leaving TJ confused. Amanda's presence was extraordinary, especially when he was expecting Kain to show up.

'Good evening, Major,' he saluted her, 'where's Kain?'

'Don't get mad, TJ,' Viper pleaded.

'Mad, why would I get mad? Amanda, why should I not be getting mad?'

'It's okay, Ashley. TJ, I sent Kain and Ann to get help for us.'

'You What? I'm sorry; I take back what I said before. You're loony! You just sent our only two Blademasters to go get help through countless miles of forest. You probably just killed the both of them. Plus, they will have no idea of where we are going to be when, and if they get back.'

'I wouldn't worry about that,' snarled a reptile with a purplish hue to its scales, 'I won't even report this to Kraston.'

At that point another reptile appeared in the firelight and deposited two armour-clad figures onto the ground.

Not ten seconds later, another creature dropped two more troopers in front of Amanda and TJ.

'Keep your people in line, Major,' the purplish one said before all three reptiles disappeared into the blackness of the forest night.

'Man they're creepy quiet,' Buzz said as he watched them leave.

'See, if they're still alive,' TJ ordered, '... and see who those other two are. I think maybe you should consult with the senior field operatives before you give another order, ma'am.'

'They're out like lights but otherwise unharmed,' Daniella said.

'And those two?' he asked.

'TJ, I'm sorry. I thought that... Well, Ann said we should at least try something,' she said through clenched teeth. Amanda was beside herself at being berated.

'Ann? Well, she's command material, isn't she? If these things had wanted to be anything less than friendly, those troopers would all be dead. The only thing Ann's little operation proved is that the reptiles want us alive for some reason.'

'It's Rich and Steve,' Dolly announced looking through the dirty visors, 'they look a little ragged but at least they get to sleep.'

'Where under Sol did they come from?' Buzz knelt to check Rich's wounds.

'Somewhere nice judging by how clean their armour is,' Viper said as she started looking over Steve's bio readouts.

'Well, small miracles! Look Amanda, I'm not sure how Daniella feels, but you will not be ordering my squad around anymore. Any orders that you feel any member of my squad should have, go through me. Clear?' TJ was mad, and he did not care what his speech cost him. He was not going to lose any more people to poorly thought-out plans.

'Yeah, clear,' she said, subdued.

'See to these people, Ken, and then get some rest. I'll pull a double shift to cover for Kain. For now though, I need some time alone,' he walked off, out of sight and towards the reptiles' camp.

*****

CHAPTER XII
Thursday, 6 April, 2251

For most of the residents on the Eden peninsula, April 6th was the start of another beautiful spring day. The welcome sun reflected perfectly with the crystals in the air creating rainbows visible all over the peninsula. In the heart of the Sky Trees, the small group of humans awoke in a foul mood, enough to rival any bad day in history. Four of them were worse off than the rest. Ann, Kain, Rich, and Steve woke up with massive headaches screaming for attention, far louder than any other body ache. Half of the packet pain killers between them and their moods improved marginally. Ann, unlike the others, failed to improve. It was more a conscious decision than anything else. She avoided looking at TJ while she packed her equipment and moved out.

The residual of the two squads was marching through the trees less than an hour after sunrise. Steve and Rich told of their day and a half adventure alone.

After Steve had jumped off the BRAT following Rich, they tumbled through the mud for what was probably a hundred feet. In the struggle with the Bregan, the blade in Rich's hand somehow found its way under the creature's chin. At the time that the creature fell, there were no other Bregan around nor was the convoy. They quickly agreed on what to do.

They knew that they would soon be outnumbered so they dug themselves into the mud and hid while the angry masses chased after the convoy. While they were lying in the mud, the Bregan returned, crawling on all fours to fight off the effects of the heavy winds, and dragged away their dead. Even under a foot of mud and below a raging storm the two were still able to hear the gargoyles' angry grunting.

They waited an hour in the mud before their environmental units began to overheat despite the water surrounding them and they had to get up. Rising slowly from their shallow graves, they sat for a short time, letting the rain wash their suits. They used this time to decide on what they were going to do next now they were totally alone. They knew the convoy had used the change in the mood of the Bregan to their advantage, heading for the only cover for miles around, the cover provided by the trees.

They would undoubtedly plan to move north the next day.

With the convoy's course determined as near as they could estimate, they rested beside the shallow graves they had previously sheltered in, to prepare for the coming day.

Shortly after dawn, they had marched on a west by northwest course towards, and eventually into the trees. They searched for three hours before finding any trace of the convoy they could follow with any degree of certainty. It was the anthill that indicated a man-made path. The large insects had taken notice of them and tried an attack but were not able to land more than a few dozen on the armour and were easily brushed off. They figured they were behind the convoy by as little as ten minutes when the Bregan jumped them.

They knew the fight was going to end badly, even though they had killed two of them. They were ready to resign themselves to defeat when the Bregan abruptly stopped fighting and flew off making that horrific noise. The two troopers were dead-tired and could do little except lean on a nearby tree for a while. Once they had their energy back, they towards the Bregan and the clearing but everyone had left. Only the bodies and wrecked vehicles remained. They continued from that point to follow the troop. The reptile creatures surprised them at sunset.

During the last hour of their trip, various members of the group informed the two new arrivals of the events that had transpired since they had fallen from the BRAT. As expected, the news Fort Grey had fallen, hit each the hardest and caused a moment of silence throughout the group.

The convoy emerged into a large clearing in the forest. Before them was a grand vision of an advanced city entirely populated by the reptile creatures. The initial extent of civil security amounted to a low black rock wall rising to a height of only four feet surrounded the city. The two towers guarding the entranceway were both ten feet high and wide enough for two reptiles to stand beside each other.

Reptilian creatures in a rainbow of colours could be seen walking inside these less than formidable barriers. As they passed through under the towers, TJ looked up to see two creatures on each tower, looking suspiciously at the lot of them and covering them with their weapons.

The main road on which they entered was randomly lined with trees, some of which were in the middle of the avenue but a trampled grass path was clear. They were forest trees used most likely to provide concealment for the buildings. The red brick and wood timbered buildings themselves were covered in living foliage, which seemed to confirm the camouflage theory.

The structures to the outer edge of the circular city were only one level high while the ring of buildings next in from the walls were two levels high. The staircase effect continued to the central structures, all of which remained at three levels high. They progressed through the city attracting curious looks from most of the citizens.

'TJ,' Buzz whispered, but received no response. 'Lieutenant Marso, check the air levels.'

When he finally heard, TJ said, 'You're right, the air is perfectly filtered for us.'

'What's that, TJ?' Daniella asked while stepping in beside him.

'We don't have to use the respirators. These plants are producing so much oxygen that we can breathe unfiltered. They're apparently blocking the particles, too.'

'That would conserve a lot of power,' she said thoughtfully.

'You got it. Everyone turn off your respirators, we need to conserve power. Might be a good idea to breathe unfiltered air for a while.'

The almost imperceptible hum of the armour's respirator motor was silenced by a pressurized hiss as visors were raised to expose the humans to the clear, oxygen-rich air. The air was still thick but the high oxygen content made it more bearable to breathe. The humans almost stopped just to breathe deeply. The scents of grass and flowering trees was intoxicating. Probably more mentally than physically, most of the humans felt refreshed. Some commenting on their new perceived reserve of energy.

TJ and Daniella moved through the city looking up and down the streets they passed while their rear escort urged them along. TJ was busy inspecting a sled-like vehicle in a large garage to his right when a Daniella pulled him around so his eyes fell on the centre of the city. It was a large impact crater with a broad path leading to a cave near the centre. Towering over the cave was what looked like the battered aft section of a starship.

Both stopped, the rear escort's angry hissing drawing the attention of the rest of the Recon troopers to the scene. They gathered around the two lieutenants to stare at a sight few on the planet had ever seen. The ship was the only thing that might have indicated a presence in the area if a low-speed aerial scout had flown over. TJ had a hunch one must have gone over at some point in all these years, probably coming down to investigate before they called it in.

After a lot of shouting and tugging, the armoured humans allowed themselves to be directed away and ushered around a corner into what looked to be a red-clay tiled parade ground. Their escort lined up in front of the two-story building that nestled itself under the shadow of the starship's hull.

Kraston stood in front of the troopers and faced a line of brilliant gold reptiles and addressed what seemed to be an honour guard. During the long opening speech, TJ noticed their escort made their way into a large building beside the shadowed structure. He assumed it was the barracks and turned to point it out to Buzz when he noticed four reptiles were carrying Johnny away to the largely wooden, three-level structure across the parade ground.

'Hey!' he shouted and began to run towards the gurney.

He had only taken six steps before three bolts from the guard took him in the legs and back. He fell hard, unconscious.

*****

CHAPTER XIII
Thursday, 6 April, 2251

Not only were the results of the salvage disappointing but the personnel losses were disturbing. Martel could have the result become bottled up inside him as usual but the incident with Smith was too much. The Commander punched the side of one of the disabled BRAT hard enough to dent the side plating and drive his point home.

'Leaving personnel behind is bad enough when they've died but when you abandon a trooper in the field because you didn't want to be out there anymore is unacceptable. Since we have no courts for a court-martial within hundreds of miles I'll save the time. Captain Ladore, for failure to execute your duty to safeguard troopers in your command you are reduced in rank to Lieutenant.'

'But sir, the threat of attack...'

'Was minimal. You had a full squad at your disposal to look for any signs of Private Smith and you chose not to. You are hereby assigned to the resupply team under Captain...'

'Resupply! But I'm a combat trooper,' she protested.

'Then you should have gone out looking to fight for *all* your people. We're done now... Lieutenant.'

The troopers within earshot stood in stunned silence at the venom of the exchange. Those further inside the camp were awed by the result of this field level court-martial. Everyone made themselves busy as Commander Martel stormed out of the encampment for some time to think and cool off.

Martel could not believe it. Not only was he losing people but now his officers were disregarding them if they became a burden. Every trooper was a bother at some point, especially officers.

'Commander!' a trooper called out. He ran to catch Martel.

'Yes, Corporal Lestton?' He tried to know all the names of his troopers. It was harder when Fort Grey still stood but was now even more important to know his people with their numbers fallen. Now he would make a list of those he had lost and add Smith to a constantly growing scroll. Someday that list would end.

'Commander, the east scouts have reported contact with individual Bregan scouts.'

'How far out?'

'Two miles at the moment. They appear to be in a search pattern and are closing in on us.'

'Okay, thanks. It's time to go,' he patted the trooper on the shoulder and led the way back.

The troopers finished the loading of equipment, supplies and personnel between the vehicles in record time despite Lieutenant Ladore pausing frequently to fire searing glares at the Commander. The supply Captain was having none of it and put more than a couple dents in her shoulder plating to get her moving.

'Private Aceves, signal the convoy to move out,' Martel said to the communication tech in the lead GCR as he took a seat in the back of the vehicle.

'Yes, sir.'

Doors slid closed as the ten remaining hovercraft moved away from the two derelict transports at N200. The dark did little to slow the vehicles or the effectiveness of the sensors but it greatly impacted on the mood of the troopers. Radar signals at the two mile mark indicated Bregan at an ever increasing frequency. A new contact appeared on the scope every other minute and they seemed to have picked up on their trail.

Commander Martel ordered the convoy to increase speed to maximum to try to clear the Brossan hills as fast as possible. Exit to the north was too risky given the squad had already been attacked in that direction. The east showed nothing but pulsing green wings closing in on them and south led them nowhere. West was the only way for now; they would turn north in a few miles.

They managed to keep clear of the Bregan force for an hour and a half before the enemy finally came into firing range. Lieutenant Carken was the first to switch focus towards the forward radar just as the first beam cannons fired into pursuers. A quick glance at the screen seemed to show it had been blocked out but as the resolution sharpened the white-out was actually a mass of enemy contact blocking their path.

'Commander! Hostiles ahead and there's a lot!' Carken cried out.

Martel quickly leaned around the gunnery chair as it whirled to track the targets behind the convoy. He clutched the console with the radar screen to absorb the meaning of the white dots. He knew the convoy weaponry could handle multiple targets focused in only one direction but now they were almost surrounded. They would have to fight outside.

'Drop the ramps! Light the blades, we have no other option,' Martel ordered.

'Yes, sir. All units deploy troops,' Private Aceves signalled.

'Keep a gunner in every chair though,' Martel yelled back from the rear hatch of the GCR.

Twenty troopers jumped out of the sleds as they slid to a halt. Their blades snapped to life instantly and they braced themselves for the coming wave. The night lit up constantly with the glow from the beam cannons and a dull glow of the blades cutting the air. The troopers did not have to wait long before the light from the Bregan's wings turned night into day.

The first attack not involving a beam cannon shot, came from the ambush group to the west with a half dozen creatures jumping onto the troopers. Blades swung franticly at first and managed to stall the attack initially. Scythes of the Bregan continued to slice at the armoured humans. Their blades stopped most of it while the armour took the remainder with cuts and scratches the result. As the minutes ticked by, the numerical odds rapidly swung from a human advantage to a vast Bregan superiority.

In a moment of fatigue, a Bregan soldier rushed at a trooper and brought him down before a blade could be brought around. He was the first casualty but not the last. These hardened troops had been fighting for a long time since the first attack on Fort Grey and were able to handle the barrage well. The constant influx of gargoyles was enough, however, to press the troopers into a tighter and tighter circle.

The next event made its own light when somehow a Bregan broke into a GCR. Short-lived screams heard over the comm. was the only warning something was wrong. When the vehicle's reactor went critical, the whole group knew exactly what happened.

The blast knocked everyone to the ground including a large group of Bregan that had no doubt thought there might be a meal being delivered by the doomed sled. Massive structural damaged also rendered one of the BRATs little more than a shell. The trooper acting as the transport's gunner was pinned in the wreck and could be heard calling for help.

The Bregan force fared badly in the blast. They did not have concussion protection the power armour of the humans, provided. Many were rendered unconscious or worse. Martel knew this was the moment he needed.

'Everyone up, load up, we're leaving,' he ordered.

The troopers did not wait to be told twice. They pushed off the ground and ran to the nearest vehicle. The trooper caught in the wrecked BRAT heard the order to withdraw but was still pinned. Commander Martel continued to order the troopers to load up even when some balked at not helping the trapped soldier.

'When those things get up, we will die. *All* of us! Get on a sled now. Pilots start moving!'

Lieutenant Ladore stopped and stared at the Commander. He had court-marshalled her for doing exactly that order. He saw her and returned the glare before firing a finger pointing her to a GCR then ducking into his sled. Ladore jumped into her sled but she would remember this point for the future trial there most certainly would be.

The new and smaller convoy took off quickly before most of the Bregan managed to get their synapses to fire in a straight line. A clean get away except for one of the ground-bound Bregan, who got a claw moving enough to grab the ankle of the last of the fleeing troopers. The soldier spun quickly and buried her blade into the head of the creature. Although that should have ended the problem, more Bregan came to and several converged on the trooper. She fought hard but was overcome while buying time for the convoy to speed away. Looks of sadness from the crew of the last GCR was the extent of assistance that could be offered.

Travel to the west was fast and silent. The cries of the trapped trooper still echoed in the fleeing sleds and killed all discussion long after the convoy was out of range. They were all tired and running on adrenaline, but hours would pass before Martel ordered the escape to cease. He used a small creek as a reference point to make camp. They would turn north after the troopers had rested.

After hours of constant attack, the troopers could not muster any energy, particularly now realizing they had left two of their number to the mercy of the enemy. Their numbers were smaller but they would deal with that in the morning. Even Lieutenant Ladore was willing to defer discussion and any complaints until first light and after a well-earned sleep.

The dim glow of actual dawn lit the dull green haze in the air. Dawn was not necessary to highlight the five Bregan sneaking up on the slumbering camp. Perimeter patrols where the first to see the sparkling eyes of the creatures as they crawled over the gravel in the creek bed. The trooper on the north side of the camp absorbed the initial attack. While he killed one Bregan, the others quickly disarmed him before delivering a series of fatal blows.

His alert was enough to jolt the camp into action and meet the advancing scouting party. Blades burst to life and seemingly every inch of the Bregan lit up. The creatures discarded their clandestine approach and rushed the encampment. Groggy actions by the rudely awakened troopers resulted in the quick death of two more troopers. More were only able to defend themselves despite outnumbering the attackers nearly seven-to-one.

Ladore was the first to score a kill as she struck a Bregan that was beating another trooper to death against the side of the sole remaining BRAT. Two more gargoyles were cut down by a stream of blue death from the number four GCR that had managed to power up after the start of the attack. The one remaining attacker clearly knew that there was no way it could make another kill and chose to take to the air. The only active turret fired at the retreating creature but failed to score a hit.

'Report! What's our status?' Commander Martel called out to no one in particular.

'We're beat worse than Bane could do, you idiot!' Ladore ripped into him.

'You're relieved, Lieutenant!' Martel fired back. 'Lieutenant Carken, check the wounded, see what can be done. Captain Penet, get the sleds fired up and secure the area!'

'Oh, now you do something, now you look after the wounded.' Ladore kept on with the verbal attack.

'That's it... Private Spel, arrest Ladore and lock her into BRAT until we get to Port Mars.'

Before the Private could place handcuffs on the Lieutenant, her reaction caught everyone by surprise. Ladore drew her blade and activated it. The troopers stepped back but were alert in the face of a danger no one had expected. Ladore slowly moved towards the north side of the camp.

'You won't be sticking me in any cage. I haven't fought this hard just to rot in a box. Commander Martel is leading all of you to an early grave, that is if anyone ever finds your bodies!'

'Ladore, you will never find safety in any outpost or city as long as I'm alive. You are a disgrace to that uniform and to everything under the sun!'

Martel calmly walked towards the armed trooper.

'Maybe but I'll be alive.' She closed her blade then backed

away from the camp.

Many troopers stared at the former Lieutenant as she walked away. Others knew what they had to do and fussed with the sleds to activate all the turrets and to deal with the troopers killed in the latest attack. A couple stood next to the Commander and watched the trooper pick her way up the creek towards Fort Saturn.

'She's full of it, Commander. You did what you had to do to get us out of an unwinnable situation. We have to warn everyone else about these creatures.' The trooper kicked a Bregan body at his feet.

'Yeah, forget her. What's our next move sir?' Private Pitsey asked.

'We need a decoy. The Bregan have managed to track us every step of the way. Let's see if we can make them track something else.'

Martel slowly turned from the mutineer to address his loyal troops.

'It should be a pretty big distraction,' Captain Penet spoke out as he patted the BRAT.

'Yes, Captain. That's the perfect thing.' Martel clapped his hands. 'Set up the BRAT and one of the GCR for autopilot. We'll shoot them to the north-east and give them something to chase.'

'Yes sir. That shouldn't be a problem. Give us twenty at least.'

'Do it. Lieutenant Sandall, get the other GCRs ready to move. Reduce the decoy fuel to ten percent; they don't need to go forever.'

'Yes sir.'

Martel stood back and watched his troopers work. The count was down to twenty-two, far too low but these were the best. He watched as they worked to prep the sleds for the mission that lay ahead of each of the vehicles. Despite the trials they had been through, they were thorough and finished in only ten minutes.

'We're set sir, all hovercraft are ready to go,' Captain Penet saluted.

'Okay, set them off and bring the perimeter team in. I want to be floating in five,' Martel said.

With sunlight sparkling through the haze and reflecting on the small creek ten feet to the west the convoy started out. The blue of the water darkened by the surrounding red rocks, gave a deceptively peaceful backdrop to the start of the day. The bodies of the Bregan left behind were the only reminder not all was peaceful.

Gunners in the six remaining GCR tracked the automated GCR and BRAT as they made their short-lived journey away from the convoy's escape route.

Martel kept the sleds pushing hard for the duration of the day. Grass wakes followed each of the escape vehicles again. The co-pilots of the vehicles took turns in reporting contact with likely Bregan scouts pacing them to the north but not making any overt moves to indicate the convoy was in any jeopardy.

'Sir, we're directly south of Fort Saturn now,' Corporal Dalar called back to the Commander.

'Okay, start to angle north twenty degrees. How are our flighty friends?'

'Only one on radar. Direction of travel indicates its moving back to the east. I think it's given up looking.'

'We'll take that as a sign. When we get to the Rim River we'll set camp on the west bank. That'll give us an hour to stretch our legs before dark.'

Finally in more than thirty hours of constant running, hiding and fighting the last troopers out of Fort Grey found to rest. Watches were set but nothing could keep the men and women laid out on the bank of the river from dropping into an almost comatose sleep. Martel could not manage the merciful bliss that was that type of darkness. He dozed fitfully, fighting off the swarm of images of the people he had lost in the past week.

Martel woke early and relieved the last watch. The predawn hour was slow to pass, like the sleep that had avoided him through the night. The entire world was black save for the small rotating radar screen. In those precious minutes alone, Martel let his mind empty and allowed the images of lost troopers fade into the surrounding darkness. By the time Captain Penet entered the GCR as the sun was rising, Commander Martel had regained the relaxed demeanour he was known for.

'Good morning, Commander,' the Captain saluted. 'Squad is waking and we've decided to have some campfire coffee.'

'Very good, Captain,' Martel said. He stretched as much as the communication station allowed. 'I think that's the best idea I've heard in a while.'

Martel stepped out of the hovercraft to a scene of cook fires contributing light to the slow glow spreading across the sky.

Troopers walked around and chatted with their visors open to enjoy the coffee and the scents in the air. These men and women savoured the joy of being alive and able to breathe. When these troopers saw that the Commander emerged from the GCR, they snapped to attention and saluted the man they had risked their lives to save from day one. He managed to return the salute professionally.

'Coffee sir?' Corporal Cranes held out a cup.

'Thank you, I am pleased to see everyone so rested.' He sipped the rather sharp brew.

'Sorry sir, we didn't have any sweetener in the supply packs.'

'Don't worry about it. Well, I think we'll take it easy today,' he started and got a few laughs, 'We are south of Forth Saturn but we have no reason to think that they haven't fallen into the same mess as we have. Therefore we are going break for New Terra since that's about as far as our fuel will last.'

'Excuse me sir, I did a few recalculations during our run last night and we should be able to make it all the way to Port Mars,' Captain Penet said.

'Wonderful! I think we'll take a drive out to the Terra Beach Resort and not have to watch the power gauge.'

The troopers clapped his speech and finished their coffee. He could tell they just wanted this trip to be over with. Their movements were still quick and maybe even quicker with a home of sorts coming into view. He drank the last of his coffee before the fires were put out and the order given to make the last push. If they ran all day they would make it to the port city a couple hours after dark.

'Keep an eye on those radar screens. We don't want anything jumping out at us.'

*****

CHAPTER XIV
Thursday, 6 April, 2251

The instant the cry from TJ rang out, nine sparkling green blades snapped to life. The four brownish coloured reptilian soldiers put Johnny down carefully and backed away. The squad of humans circled the two unconscious men and kept their blades at the ready. A steady stream of reptiles flowed into the parade ground to circle the squad but whether civilian or military was not clear. Dozens upon dozens of shining rifles were quickly trained on each of the human blades. The only move each of the men and women made was to close their visors and seal their armour.

Kraston pushed his way through the lines to survey the situation. He knew the humans would die if a firefight started and that situation was not to be permitted.

'Crimson and silver guard, return to your posts. Gold guard, lower your weapons,' he boomed.

Amazingly and without question, the reptiles of the various guards did exactly as they were told. Such a level of discipline was foreign to the humans who remained alert for possible trickery.

'Please, friends, lower your crystal swords. There is no harm for you here. Allow my medical staff to tend to your comrades,' he spoke soothingly.

These humans are an interesting lot, thought Kraston while he smiled at the troopers, protective of their own and more than anxious to fight. But more than anything, they are fast and cunning – a deadly combination indeed. They might end up being very useful.

'Won't you join me for something to eat?' he offered pleasantly.

His charms were working, at least for now. The female leader lowered her blade and ordered the rest to follow suit. As soon as the blades were deactivated, eight of his medics rushed in to carry the two injured humans to recovery beds. Several watched suspiciously as the men were carried away while others kept an eye on the surrounding creatures.

'Perhaps you would care to freshen up a little bit before we eat?' The charm was being laid on thick now.

'Yes,' the female said, 'that would be great.'

'Excellent. Please, follow my guards to a bedding-house. Rooms have been secured for all of you.'

'Thank you, Kraston,' she said graciously.

Kraston disappeared into the compound complex under the shadow of the wrecked ship while his gold guards took the humans to the bedding house. They would remain there while he made his plans as to what to do with them. He needed time to study these odd animals before he acted.

With the arrival of the Bregan on this world as well, life would become a lot more difficult. Using these humans, Kraston could get the balance of power to move in his favour. The problem – these humans may be too few in number and they were definitely too intelligent to attack the Bregan just because he said so.

Bane, *the bringer of death*, was the only star in the sky when Buzz and Kain were shown to their room, meaning it was two hours until dusk and supper. A real meal would be a welcome thing after two days of dry rations. The guard had made a point to mention power armour would not be necessary while in the city.

'I'm not sure about this, Paul,' Buzz said.

'Relax Bill. If they wanted us dead, we would be paste at the centre of their parking lot back there,' he replied. He unhooked his helmet.

'I guess, you notice he didn't say our blades wouldn't be necessary.'

'You're nuts,' Kain laughed.

'It is odd that they have a hotel in this city,' Buzz said, disconnecting his gloves. 'I mean who are they expecting to stay?'

'Maybe they have other towns.'

'Oh that's great. How many do you think are out there and why haven't we seen any of them before today?'

'Man, I didn't even know this forest was more than a footnote in a text until today.' Kain tossed his chest plate to the floor.

'Well, that just proves you're no Christopher Columbus.'

They both talked as they shed their armoured skins for civilian clothing, which was stored in a tight bundle in the armour's pack. They were ready to go anywhere other than the small two-bed room. By D600 hours, one hour before sunset, Buzz got up from his bed and walked to the window. He had a perfect view of the ruined ship.

'I'd love to get a look inside that,' he said softly.

Kain gave a quizzical hmm, loud enough to be heard but in a tone indicating that he was not paying any attention at all. Buzz turned around to see what he was doing. Kain had risen up from the bed, crept to the door and was peering out into the hall.

'There are two of those gold guards at the top of the stairs. Hold on, someone's just left their room. It's Daniella – damn, she's lookin' good,' he whispered.

'Yeah, I second that,' Buzz said, peering past Kain.

'They turned her back. Looks like we really are prisoners.'

'I think these lizards know more about us than they're letting on.'

'But not enough,' Kain smiled, 'How 'bout you and I take a look at that ship of theirs. Put your armour back on, we'll probably need it.'

'I think it'd be safer if we just stay put,' Buzz said hesitantly. He still moved to put on his armour.

In minutes they were suited up and standing by the door listening to the guards. When he decided they were well and truly engrossed in their conversation, Kain signalled Buzz to move to the window. Buzz hung out the window while Kain climbed down his back to the ledge of the next window. He looked in to make sure no one would see him before steadying himself and letting Buzz in turn climb down his back.

Once Buzz was hanging from the second floor window he pushed off the wall and dropped to the ground. Kain quickly followed in the same fashion. When they were sure they had made it to the ground undetected, they crawled north to the crater of the ship in failing light. They pushed their way through two foot tall grass that seemed stiffer than typical foliage. Kain and Buzz used their night vision HUD to avoid the guards on patrol and managed to get to the crimson walled cave at the base of the ship without tripping any alarms. They waited until the guards turned away from their route before scurrying inside the non-terrestrial starship.

Daniella paced the room she shared with Sam, her civilian clothes flapping in the wake of her hurried pace. She wore a sleeveless white blouse and black cotton stretch-leggings. She also had a long dress coat in a dark charcoal grey that lay draped on chair next to the door. It was fancier than the others' casual clothes, she liked to show off a bit.

What she did not like was the fact they were confined to their rooms, and segregated. It definitely did not feel right. She needed to think of a way out and she had always thought best while she paced. After ten laps around the room, she stopped at the window and bent her head slightly.

'By the light!' she muttered.

'Oh, come on, Daniella,' Sam said. Smiling, she stood up, 'It's not hopeless. I mean, we'll think of something.'

'What are you talking about, girl?'

'You,' she said approaching the window. She put her arm around Daniella's shoulder, 'Hanging your head and sighing like you've given up.'

Daniella laughed, 'I wasn't sighing for us. I was muttering at those two sneaking through the grass.' She pointed at the armoured shadows slinking away.

'Who...' started Sam before she recognized the pair, 'That's Kain and Buzz – they're mad!'

'Looks like we'll have to help the men again. Come on,' and the women headed out the door.

Almost as soon as they stepped through the threshold, two gold guards descended on them, shouting orders to remain in the room. At the same moment, Dolly and Erik stepped out of their room to check on the raucous. The guards stopped their talking and levelled their weapons at the two groups.

'Hey, whoa fella!' Dolly put his hands up.

'Easy now,' Daniella said.

'Get back in your rooms,' one of the guards ordered.

'What's going on here?' Amanda asked, storming out of her room with Ann in tow, blade in hand, although it was turned off. They had appeared in the hall behind the guards.

'We need help up here,' said a guard into a radio pad he wore, once it realized they were surrounded.

The sound of hurried footsteps could be heard thundering up the staircase before four more guards burst onto the scene. The odds would have been evened except for Steve, Rich and Ashley emerging from their room, once again, behind the guards. Tension was high and it was clear the reptiles were nervous.

'I said back in your rooms, warm bloods!' the guard snapped with authority. He was visibly shaking.

'Amanda, we're just worried about TJ and Johnny,' Daniella said.

'And these things are acting as if we're prisoners,' Sam added.

'Alright,' Amanda said to calm the troopers before turning to the guards, 'Would you mind explaining why we can't go outside like we were promised or even check on our fellow troopers?'

'That's the order... ma'am.' It sneered at the last part.

At that moment an energy bolt seared the air past Amanda's head and took a large chunk out of the wall behind her. None of the humans saw where it had come from – in fact the guards looked stunned by the shot as well. The results were immediate, three troopers took up positions around Amanda despite her protests. The remaining troopers arranged themselves into another group. The second each of the formations was formed, seven blades snapped to life.

If the reptiles were nervous before, it was obvious now. Bolt rifles versus blades was one thing in the open field, but bolt versus blade in a confined hall was quite another. They were really nervous now.

'Now that we have your attention,' Daniella winked at Sam, 'how about you get your boss up here to explain why we are prisoners without actually being told about charges.'

The guards hesitated before the one closest to the stairs ran, with unbelievable speed, for the lowers levels of the bedding house. They assumed it was going for the guards' commander. Both groups remained at the ready just in case either side felt the necessity to attack. With Amanda in the group, the reptiles knew the humans could get the order at any second.

Time seemed to grind extremely slowly at fear's edge, honing it. Minutes passed since the guard had left and neither side had budged an inch. Slowly, a conversation started through the glimmering of blades and under the harsh stare of the bolt rifle's muzzle.

As the discussion progressed, muzzles were lowered and blades were deactivated. In the twenty minutes it had taken the guard to return with Kraston, all tension in the groups had been alleviated and the weapons were put away.

The guards discussed various topics with the Recon troopers in group, or one on one conversations. Jests were tossed around, with several explanations in the translations. The fact that these things could speak the same language as the humans helped. There were some vocal and opinionated discussions as well.

Kraston stood at the head of the stairs and smiled, while the guard remained bewildered beside him with his rifle ready for the fight to start. 'This will work much better,' Kraston said softly, 'I'll have my troops and citizens casually extract the necessary information from these humans.' He chuckled quietly.

'Sir?' queried the guard slowly looking around in awe.

'Go and mingle,' Kraston whispered to the guard, '... and sling that rifle.'

Kraston waited and watched for a few minutes at the easy exchange of potentially useful information. It was quite conceivable one of these humans could let slip the piece of information he needed.

'My guests, please, let me apologize for your treatment thus far. There seems to have been a mix-up in protocol. Please join me across the street in the tavern for some refreshments,' he cut off some conversations with his announcement. Despite his apparent good intentions, his interruption was not well received.

The members of the two species followed Kraston down the staircase and out of the bedding house to a triangular three-storied structure at the corner of the next block. Drinks and food were ordered while talks on several subjects continued into the night.

All the while, Kraston watched like a snake eyeing a blind mouse, smiling quietly. He talked little but remembered everything he heard. Recording instruments around the establishment would ensure he missed nothing.

*****

CHAPTER XV
Thursday, 6 April, 2251

Kain and Buzz carefully negotiated their way through the roughly dug tunnel while the others made nice with their captors. Because the tunnel was only dimly lit, they had to continue to use the light-enhancing optics of their suits to avoid stone or construction debris that might announce their presence. The path dove steeply to the point where they now had to use their hands to better hold their position as they hunted for footholds.

'I think they tunnelled through Mars,' Buzz joked half seriously.

'I'll be writing a letter if they did. I do not want to live on a ventilated planet, thank you very much!' Kain quipped back. 'Do we even know if this tunnel goes anywhere?'

'They wouldn't have been guarding it if it didn't, would they? Hey man, see anything besides Martian bedrock yet?'

'Not yet, just watch your step. Whoa! What's this? Hold up.'

'What cha got?' Buzz froze and checked the path up and down to see if they had company. Being the lower of the two armoured men, Kain was the first to encounter a rust-speckled metal hull-plate making up the floor and one wall of a cavernous opening beside the ship. The light was better next to the hull thanks to the reflections of their head lamps, enough to allow them to have a better look around once they were magnetically clamped to the hard floor. They were able to walk ten feet away from the tunnel opening before they found the entrance-way on the floor.

It was an improvised door not a standard hatch, welded into an outward-facing blast hole. The welds were strong and managed to seal the seams well, though the odd jagged edge protruded. Of course being *welded* to the hull of the ship and spanning ten feet across meant that being side by side next to a panel Kain and Buzz were actually standing on the door. Kain tried to step off the portal, only succeeding in triggering the opening mechanism. Caught completely off guard, they plummeted into the ship when the hatch popped open inward.

Physics took over, falling despite their magnetic boots. Their fall turned into a skid along the wall when it came up behind them at an angle of twenty-degrees off the vertical. The skid lasted ten seconds, at which point they found themselves stuck to the wall.

Kain stayed on his back for the time being, 'Ooops...'

'Yeah, how about I lead from now on?' Buzz stated calmly.

'Okay.' He paused, 'So leader, fearless or otherwise, what do we do now?'

'Well...' Buzz lifted his head to look around. When he relaxed his neck his helmet snapped back against the *wall*. 'Either the wall is magnetized or we are lying on the deck of the ship.'

'Let's just test that theory,' Kain suggested before he pushed himself to his feet.

Instead of falling as one would have expected, he stood perfectly perpendicular to the *wall* and looked down on Buzz.

'Looks like they know about artificial gravity generators. Which means that while we're on this ship, I'm upright and you're laying your heavy ass on the floor,' he smiled.

'Nice,' Buzz said. Kain offered his hand to lift him up. 'Now let's see what we've gotten ourselves into.'

Looking around, they saw they had ended up in a dull yellowish hallway with a bend in front of them and to the right. The hall stretched behind them to a distance of ten feet, maybe more until it too went around a corner to the left. There were three doors on the left hand wall, one at either end of the short corridor and the last in the middle.

'Looks like my primary school.'

'Let's see what's behind door number one,' Kain said.

They moved in front of the door and pressed the touch pad to open it. Behind the thick blast-grade metal door was a large room looking similar to a targeting control room of a beam cannon turret, like the one in Fort Grey. The controls were in a language other than Terran Standard and they had no hope of translating without the proper equipment. Their basic functions could be guessed at with some work.

'All the read-outs show red. I'm guessing that means they're off-line,' Kain noted.

'The systems were probably knocked out in the crash,' Buzz said scanning the damaged control panel.

'Good to see they haven't been transferring these components to the surface. That means they probably won't have any anti-armour weapons up there,' Kain speculated as they moved out of the control room.

'Their rifles seem to work well enough for that.'

They came out and looked down the side passageway after re-entering the hall. The passage maintained a ten foot width and extended thirty feet before it turned to the left. In the corner they saw another door that had been propped open for some reason.

'Well, that looks like an open invite, eh?' Buzz said as he tapped Kain's chest plate and stepped towards the room.

'Welcoming... like an alligator's jaws.' Kain moved ahead of him and readied his blade in an eruption of glowing shards.

Buzz's blade activated a second later, illuminating the passageway in a monochrome hue. Beyond what sparse lighting was provided by Buzz's blade, Kain stepped to the left wall and peered around the corner. The hall extended for two hundred feet, poor lighting and the grey colouring of this hall made it hard to tell the full length with any accuracy. At a point forty feet down the hall another hallway branched off to the right.

He did not see anyone, it seemed to all too quiet. A quick hand signal from Kain sent Buzz across the hall through the doorway at a run. He scurried behind a computer bank that provided sufficient cover and scanned the room. He gestured to Kain with an all-clear signal when he was sure the room was secure.

Kain peeked around the corner the moment before he ran across the hall into the doorway. That precautionary measure allowed him to remain undetected by the red guard now walking down the corridor towards his position. He motioned to Buzz to take cover and switched off his blade as he melted into the shadow of a shallow bend in the wall that was dark enough to hide him from anything with the exception of a direct look.

The guard came to the corner a moment later and stopped to look into the room where Buzz was now hiding behind the computer terminal. The red-scaled guard evidently saw nothing amiss and turned to walk past Kain. It took only two steps beyond Kain's hiding spot when something must have caught its eye.

The reptile whirled around to face Kain and brought its rifle to bear. Before it could fire it froze in position, its mouth hanging open as if to scream, though no sound came from its gaping jaw. Kain put his hand on the scaly shoulder and pushed away the body as he withdrew his blade.

'Give me a hand here, Buzz,' he said calmly.

Buzz emerged from the room and checked the hall for any more guards as the body finally went limp in Kain's arms. The rifle made a disturbingly loud clunk when it hit the floor plate.

Buzz picked up the weapon when he came beside Kain and helped to pull the dead reptile into the computer room. They found a large cabinet a couple of feet from the doorway large enough to conceal the body and proceeded to stuff it in awkwardly. After closing the metal door, they used a blade to disfigure the door enough to seal it.

'Hopefully, no one will find that fella for a while,' Kain said.

'I don't think we have much to worry about on that score. It looks like they're done in here.'

'What do you mean?' Kain said looking around the room, 'I don't see anything.'

'Exactly! Look on the floor. There, and there.' Buzz said pointing to various spots. 'There are scrape marks and heavy denting all over the place.'

'Oh yeah, I see it... that means that there was some stuff in here and it got moved out. The spot where this last terminal is sitting is the same size as those empty spots. I think that this may be an access point for the main computer bank of the ship. What are you doing?' Kain asked nervously when Buzz started to access the terminal.

'They act as if they know a lot about us humans. I just want to find out a bit about them,' he smiled.

'Be quick about it!' Kain moved to the door and scanned the corridor.

'Just about got it, I think. It's weird. They seemed to have edited the programs so that their computer language is almost the same as ours. It feels like a scene in a movie involving *Star Trek's Universal Translator*.'

'You watch too many of those old movies.'

'I don't watch enough. They're our history man.'

'Oh crap... I hear something! I think we left a door open. Shhhh... They're coming!' Kain ran over to Buzz and grabbed his shoulder, 'Come on, man!'

'Give me a second,' he strained against Kain's pull. 'Got it. Go, go, go!' he said as he pulled out a disk drive from the console and took off after Kain.

They ran out of the room making heavy thuds on the metal flooring and hooked right, down the hall presumably towards the front of the ship. As they went past the branch in the hall, an emerald shot blasted across their hall and through the door behind them.

Determined not to get shot, they managed to get into another yellowish common area at the end of the hall without any more weapon fire. There was an elevator system to their right and a lot of tables in the middle of the floor.

'This looks like a mess hall,' Buzz scanned the room.

Kain stopped at the corner and ushered Buzz towards the elevator while he looked back down the hall for signs of pursuit. Instead of running after them, the crimson guard had come up a parallel hall and streamed around the opposite corner. It was down to a contest of reflexes when Buzz and the guard came face-to-visor.

Buzz had almost completely forgotten he was carrying the slain guard's bolt rifle, but he reflexively brought up the weapon as he had seen the heroes do in many of those movies. He was not used to this style of combat so his shot was let loose earlier than it should have been and went well low of its mark, the reptile's head. Still, the bolt took the guard in its right front knee and brought it down. Buzz fired again and silenced the guard before it could call for help.

Kain turned around in time to see the second bolt end the guard. 'We're going to turn this place into a morgue if we don't get out of here soon.' he said as he picked up the second bolt rifle.

'I could get used to one of these,' Buzz admired the weapon.

'I'll get you one for your birthday.'

'Help me stuff red-boy here into that forward thrust room or whatever that room is.' He read the sign across the common area as best he could.

They made it across the room in no time. Kain left his role of supporting the left side of the guard to go on ahead to open the door. He was reaching for the door when a jade bolt smashed into the wall in front of the dead guard and Buzz. The blast separated Buzz and the guard and sent them both flying to the ground. Kain broke into a run, even before Buzz hit the ground. He made it to Buzz's side and helped him into the elevator across the common room. Other guards could be heard coming up both side halls before the doors closed on them.

'Maybe they didn't see us,' Buzz puffed.

'Maybe, but I think they did. There will be too many other unexplained events. They'll know someone else was here.'

'You mean like guards dying?' Buzz asked.

'Yeah, like that.'

The elevator door whisked open and a computerized voice

announced they were now on the ninth level, surprisingly they could understand. They stepped out of the lift to face the left side of the ship. To their right was the entrance to what looked like the bridge judging by the computer layout and the smashed windows now showing only dark red rocks. On the left was another of the long hallways. The door behind them whisked shut again and the indicator beside the door showed the elevator's decent to the eighth floor. Presumably, the guards had agreed with Kain's analysis of the scene and would soon be upon them.

'Let's go onto the control centre,' Buzz suggested.

'They'd look there, I am sure I would. We don't have time to get to the end of the hall so we need to go elsewhere.' He paused to look around, 'There... that second door on the right.'

The troopers ran for the door, got through and managed to close it seconds before two green guards emerged from the elevator. Muffled conversation could be heard but nothing specific could be picked out initially. The guards' movements could be heard moving cautiously towards the control centre ... and in the process slowly advancing on the room where Kain and Buzz were hiding. As they walked past the room, some of their words filtered through the door.

'... mean, I shot him? You fired first,' one of them said with a throaty hiss.

'I'm a lousy shot so it must have been you,' the voice seemed almost feminine.

'I suppose it doesn't matter. Just tell me again why we're still looking around?'

'Because that guy you waxed dropped his gun somewhere. Now we gotta find it.'

'I told you, I didn't shoot him...'

'Not unlike junior academy, eh Kain?' Buzz smiled.

The guards moved down the hall, relaxing into an obviously unconcerned stride. Buzz pictured them walking side by side with their rifles slung over their shoulders. Five minutes later, he opened the door a crack, to make sure all was clear. When he glanced back towards the elevator, he saw the two guards turning left into another part of the ship. Kain pulled him back inside to keep him from being spotted.

'What the hell are you trying to do, you moron, get our clocks cleaned?' Kain said irritably.

'Well, you have been a little slow lately, big guy,' Buzz

responded.

'Funny. Listen, I've decoded some of that file you acquired and I found out some interesting stuff. Firstly, they call themselves Landran. Their social status is based on their colour and their rank within those classes is signified by a tattoo on their hoods.'

'Sounds like the makings of a welcoming speech. So how do they know so much about us?'

'It is a speech. I don't know how you found it, but it gives us what we were after. As for the source of their information, there was a manned space flight that impacted into this here colony ship. The Landran downloaded what they could from the Terran ship and rescued the one surviving crew member. They are masters of adaptation, apparently. In two weeks the entire conscious crew had learned English and most of our technology.'

'So you're saying that we're screwed,' Buzz moaned.

'As I was about to say, the survivor is on board but the pilot was badly injured. They put him or her in stasis because they didn't know enough about our physiology to repair the damage. I guess they knew that they would meet up with a human colony at some point.'

'Good thing they didn't land on Earth,' Buzz smiled.

'That's the odd thing. I think you missed some of the speech. There is no mention of why they crashed or where they came from.'

'Let's figure out where and why later, Sherlock, and concentrate on getting us out of this mess.'

'Yeah, hey, do you think we should get the survivor on the way out?'

'Sounds good. Hand me a flash ball, will ya?'

Kain dislodged a sphere roughly the size of a tennis ball from the underside of his pack and passed it to Buzz. It was the last combat device to come out of the Miles Research Station before the facility was destroyed two years ago.

Buzz stepped back to the door and opened it a crack. He noticed the guards had returned and decided to play it safe. When he was sure they were not looking he activated the timer and rolled the flash ball towards them. He watched as the ball rolled to a stop four feet from the Landran and detonated.

The expanding dull-blue field vaporized the ball before it solidified to its matter-resistant state and impacted into the sides of the guards at more than two hundred miles-per-hour. For a brief second, the pair was pinned against the walls before the field ran out of power and dissipated. They slumped to the floor, unconscious.

'They're down,' Buzz whispered. He led the way into the hall.

In the dead silence of the ship's hull, their running footsteps resounded deafeningly. They ran past a hallway on the left and came to a halt when another set of elevators appeared on the right.

'Down?' Buzz asked.

'Yeah, two levels, then we'll come back this way then go up one level and get out.'

'Good plan,' he said stepping into the elevator car.

Kain jumped in right behind him. 'I'll keep the other flash ball ready just in case someone gets too curious.' He switched the fuse setting to *impact*.

They took the elevator down to the seventh level. Unlike on the upper two levels, the second bank of lifts was not here. Buzz decided they would not use the same elevator to go back up for fear of being trapped, instead they moved towards the front of the ship yet again. They went down a narrow hallway and through a pair of airlock-style doorways and into a massive room. They stood motionless, stunned by the sight before them.

Row upon row of five-high stacks of cyrochambers towered throughout this almost endless room. Nitrogen clouds hung everywhere making it impossible to see more than ten feet ahead. The clouds seemed to have a jamming effect on the suit's sensors, they were useless. Blindly moving forward through the paths between the columns was the only method of progress, more than once coming to a dead end.

Kain's sense of direction was the only thing keeping them from becoming hopelessly lost in this maze of sleeping Landran. Buzz had long since given up trying to figure out where he was when a solid wall emerged out of the noxious fog. They worked their way along the barrier until they found a hatchway. They hoped it was not the hatch that they had entered through, but it was not the hatch they had entered from. The bad news was, they knew it because this hatch was locked.

'Force it,' Buzz suggested.

Kain snapped on his blade, which emitted a hiss as uncounted numbers of nitrogen atoms were reduced to even smaller atomic components.

He easily slipped his blade along both sides of the door to

sever any locking mechanisms. There was not much time to pull his blade free before the door fell away with a powerful boom. The air inside the door blasted outward and wiped away the fog, allowing them to see inside clearly.

Beyond the door was a small room, partially collapsed. The damage appeared to have been caused in the crash leaving a small space and another hatch. In the section of room that remained was a single tubular cryochamber. They walked up beside it and Kain brushed away a thin layer of ice.

'Man, its cold in here. Did I thank you yet for making me take this suit with me?' Buzz asked.

'No you didn't,' Kain smiled, wiping the last of the crystals clear to reveal the occupant of the chamber. 'Damn, it's a woman, from the hips up at least.'

'What?' Buzz looked into the chamber, 'where's the rest of her?'

'I would guess that's the injury they couldn't heal.'

'How do we get her out? The instant she's out of there her stats would drop like a stone. Then we'll really need a medic!'

'I don't know, maybe...' Kain stopped. 'Someone's coming. Quick, out the other door.'

The last thing they heard before the door closed behind them was a Landran make an obscene reference to the construction quality of the door. Using helmet-mounted lights, they moved down a narrow hallway. After ten feet, debris began to appear on the floor. Soon they were climbing over mounds of framing and plate steel with the occasional clump of red soil. The troopers worked their way through the increasing rubble until the ceiling met the top of the unnatural hill.

'Now what?' Buzz asked.

'I'd think, go there.' He pointed to a broken and partially crushed tube protruding from the ceiling. 'That my friend, looks suspiciously like an elevator tube.'

They climbed over the wreckage to the tube and forced the opening large enough to squeeze through. They worked their way up the tube to the eighth level door. While Kain supported him, Buzz used his blade to force the door open. When the door was open an inch, he saw the back of a red Landran guard.

He assumed there would be two of them, signalling Kain for the second flash ball.

He pried the door open enough to slide his arm through. He

was putting his arm through the opening when the guard casually looked behind him, perhaps hearing Buzz's efforts. He was stunned to see an armoured arm protruding from the hatchway.

When the armoured hand tossed a small metal sphere into the air, the guard jumped for it reflexively. While he managed to catch the ball, he overbalanced himself and fell with the ball beneath him. The energy pulse sent the guard straight up into the ceiling while at the same time tossed the second guard through the thrust room door directly across from the elevator.

Buzz and Kain pried the warped doors and stepped out of the lift tube after the two bodies settled to the floor and ran to the right and around the corner. Three-quarters of the way down the hall, a green Landran stopped in front of them. Out of the weapons, Kain opted to use his fist to take out the guard.

After leaping past the falling guard, they made a quick left, then right, before running past another set of elevators and right around the lifts to stop short of the entrance hatch of the ship. Kain chanced a look around the corner to check for guards. He saw none and signalled Buzz to follow him out. Once through the door, they stumbled and almost fell when the gravitational pull reverted back to the planet. From there, they carefully edged their way out of the tunnel and back to their room in the bedding house.

'I have no idea how you managed to find that exit,' Buzz said as he clambered through the window.

'Would you believe it if I said I had a photographic memory?' Kain smiled.

'Not a chance.'

They changed quickly into their civilian clothes and found a holographic chessboard to make themselves seem occupied. Five minutes later, a gold Landran guard opened their door, surprised to see them.

Confused, he asked, 'Where did you come from?'

'Hey, man, you're blowing our concentration here,' Buzz said angrily.

'Ah, sorry. The rest of your group is still across the street if you care to join them.'

Smiling, Buzz and Kain stood. 'That sounds like a great idea, friend; show us the way!'

While at the dinner with their companions, Buzz and Kain

relayed some of their experiences with the group in return for whatever information the rest have discovered about their hosts. The two managed to relax and enjoy themselves, in spite of the adventure they had experienced.

*****

CHAPTER XVI
Friday, 7 April, 2251

A low, strained moan permeated every foot of the recovery wing of the medical building situated at the north end of the compound. The source of the moan was TJ. The sound indicated he was awake but that he would have preferred not to be.

The throbbing pain in his back spiked with every movement while the ache in his head cried out for attention almost constantly. Near as he could figure, he was in one piece which at least pleased him. An hour ago he had decided to look out the window at the late morning landscape, now it was after noon and he had only gotten as far as throwing his sheets back.

'Up we go now,' he mumbled to himself, straining against the numb feeling his joints had unanimously adopted. He struggled into a seated position with his legs hanging over the side of his bed. He had to stop at that point to catch his breath.

'This is ridiculous,' he whined to himself.

'Pathetic is the word I would have used,' a voice behind him commented.

TJ slowly turned his head around causing his world to spin around him. The effort made him nauseous though he was able to tolerate it. His eyes settled on the form of Johnny Gentry standing at the door to his room. Johnny was dressed in his civilian clothes but otherwise looked good. TJ smiled despite the effort required.

'Sir,' Iceman added.

'That's better. How are you?'

'Got a big headache, but otherwise good. ...Sir, I thought we were supposed to be fighting these creatures.'

'I'm a bit fuzzy on that point myself.' TJ groaned at the effort required to stand, 'They shot me up pretty good, so who knows.'

He stood for a moment regaining his strength before shuffling his way to the window. Iceman joined him to stare at the foliage-covered buildings and the small green-space between them.

'Any idea how long we've been here boss?' Johnny asked.

'Here? Just one night, I think, but you've been out for almost two days, if I'm right.'

'Two days ...Damn. I don't remember anything.'

'Let's get out of this hole then I'll tell you what happened since you went out to it.'

'The director of this *hole* has decided that since you are both mobile, you are to be released from our care,' a green creature said with disdain. The nurse left in a huff.

'Cool!' Johnny said.

Smiling, TJ turned his gaze out the window again before he decided to get dressed. Before returning he caught a glimpse of metal in a place where only grass should have been. He knew little about architecture, human or reptilian, but something about the piece of metal was wrong. He turned away anyway and dressed as fast as his numb body could move.

'Who put the burr in your saddle?'

'We've got a mystery to solve. It's probably a drink can or something,' TJ was almost completely focused on dressing.

'They must've hit you in head 'cuz you ain't makin' any sense there, chief.'

'Trust me, I'm fine. Get armoured and meet me out front.'

'Okay then,' Johnny saluted casually.

TJ stepped out of the medical building into an assault of sunlight, fresh air and lots of activity. Green, grey and gold reptiles were on the move for as far as he could see down the streets and between the buildings. They appeared to be running a search pattern, though for what was anyone's guess. Panning around, TJ saw three grey coloured guards talking aggressively with Iceman. They all looked over to TJ when Iceman pointed, then they had a few more quick words and bustled off.

TJ walked over to Master Sergeant Gentry and whispered to him, 'So, what's up with them, bud?'

'I'm guessing that they believed one or both of us broke into that starship of theirs and did some damage, killed some guards and/or stole something. I'm not sure, but anyway, I told them we were released by the medical director maybe a half an hour ago.'

'Well, let's just hope everyone else is able to provide as good an alibi.'

'By the way this place is jumping, I'd say that they have,' he smiled.

'Good, while we have a moment let's go have a look at that

something I saw from my window,' TJ said secretively.

'Oh right, your mystery thing; gotcha,' Iceman clicked his tongue.

'Come on, smartass.'

They moved slowly around the corner of the medical building to the greenbelt between that building and the next structure leading to the small field where the fragment of metal was located. TJ was relieved to be in his power armour again. He slouched as much as his suit would allow and basically let the armour do the movement.

Occasionally, a guard would watch to keep tabs on them, but since the two men appeared to not be doing anything wrong, the guards took no further action. They finally entered what had looked like the field he had seen from the medical room window, but it was a small crater not a field. The piece of metal was on the far side of the rim of the crater. If this was the impact crater of a ship rather than a meteor strike then that spot would be where the debris would have ended up, judging by the lines in the ground anyway. They walked carefully across the indentation towards the metal fragment.

'You think that there's a hidden message in the fact we keep walking into craters?' Iceman asked, calmly scanning the surrounding area.

'None that I see,' TJ replied without looking up.

'Maybe it's just me then.'

TJ hiked up the slight incline at the far side of the shallow crater to two feet from where the metal protruded from the ground. The visible part had a surface area of two square yards and protruded as if it were an atmospheric control surface. Though whatever it was attached to was covered in a few years of dirt and vegetation, the markings on the piece were clear. It belonged to a human airship.

'This could be that Hummingbird that went missing a while back, remember?' asked Iceman.

'No, sorry. When was this?' TJ said, puzzled.

'Three years ago a Hummingbird scout hovercraft out of Port Mars was on a routine mineral expedition when it disappeared. No trace was ever found. This could be it.'

'And if it made this hole, then our *friends* must have brought it down.'

'That would answer a few questions like how we haven't seen

these things 'til now.'

'Let's regroup. It's clear that these things aren't as nice as they seem. We still have to get to Fort Saturn anyway.'

They made their way back to the main compound and identified themselves to a gold guard as the two medical patients recently released. They asked for the directions to the bedding house where the rest of the squad was located.

Both received odd looks from the various levels of guards when they entered the bedding house because of their armour even though their visors were open, indicating to other troopers at least, they were not ready to fight. Inside the bedding house they were directed to the third level, which seemed to be solely dedicated to the accommodation of the First and Second Recon squads. Once on the top floor, the two armoured men went to Amanda and Ann's room. They rapped loudly and got an immediate answer complete with two drawn blades.

'Why so jumpy, Major?' Iceman asked, putting his hands up defensively.

'Nice to see you too, ladies,' TJ smiled, although he was less than pleased at the warmth, or apparent lack thereof, of his welcome back to the land of the living.

'Oh, I'm so sorry... Hi, come in,' Amanda gave TJ a lengthy hug that was much more enthusiastic than anything he had expected from her.

'Too bad for the armour being in the way,' he muttered.

'Sorry, what?' A pale rose colour stained her cheeks.

'Nothing, nothing. Listen, can we talk here?' he asked seriously.

'Sure, everyone else should listen in too. Ann, please fetch the others.'

'Yes, ma'am,' Ann snapped a formal salute, marching out.

'I see a little of me in her, actually,' Amanda frowned.

'That's a nice way of saying it,' TJ continued to smile.

Iceman almost burst out laughing at the comment and had an even tougher time controlling himself when Amanda's face showed her irritation. Everyone already in the room remained silent while the rest of the two squads entered. Iceman was still smiling to himself as they filed in, which drawing a few raised eyebrows. Buzz and Kain had obviously been expecting something judging by their armoured presence.

'Everyone sit down, on the floor if you have to. We've got to make some travel plans,' TJ said in his best command voice then quickly glancing at his XO.

Amanda took over, 'To start, I'm sure by now everyone knows about Buzz and Kain's little adventure last night.' She paused for the applause and hooting to die down before continuing.

'Please no flowers,' Buzz stood and bowed.

'Sit down fool,' Kain smiled.

'And... we are all pleased with the results if not the means. Buzz, will you fill these two in on what you've learned about our hosts?' She moved to her seat near the window.

Buzz stood by the door and addressed the room. He gave a brief summary of the events of last night, omitting the part about killing some of the guards. He told them the information contained on the speech disk, finally details regarding the deep space crew member on board the Landran ship.

'So they're called Landran then?' Johnny asked.

'Yeah and those other things are Bregan,' Buzz finished.

'We've got to get her out then, right?' Steve interrupted.

'Weren't you listening, her legs have been torn off. If we remove her from stasis, she dies,' Kain said.

'Paul's right. We'll have to leave her here. As for us, it'll take hours before the Landran commander will see us, if they used the same command procedures as the little incident in the hall yesterday. So this is what's going to happen. First, everyone suit up and meet in the hallway. Then we walk out of this place and hopefully rendezvous with Commander Martel's squad on route to Port Mars,' Major Harte announced.

Those not already in their armour filed out of the room to get ready for another journey and Amanda kicked the rest out so she and Ann could get into their suits. Out in the hall, TJ and three armoured troopers milled around and made idle conversation.

'What on Mars are you doing suited up, Buzz?' he asked as soon as the door closed.

'Had a feeling you'd be awake today and things always get interesting when you're awake,' Buzz smiled broadly.

'Awesome,' Kain chuckled and fist bumped the trooper.

'I've been wanting to ask you, TJ,' Iceman started

'What's that, bud?' TJ asked while he adjusted some settings in his suit.

'What exactly are these things on my arms?'

'Your hands?' TJ smiled before he looked up.

The other two troopers, Buzz and Kain, burst into laughter. Iceman stepped forward and walloped the back of TJ's helmet.

'Uh, sorry man,' TJ said while he recovered from the hit, 'Those are the newest defensives component on our suits courtesy of Mister Ken Michelson. They are proximity activated blades mounted in opposing fashion to create a force field similar to the assault screens of the Crystal City.'

'Um, okay.' Iceman looked confused.

'Hold out your arm.' TJ said. When he complied, a familiar faint hiss filled the hall as TJ activated his blade and slowly brought it close to Iceman's arm. At a distance of three inches, two emerald green beams shot forward from their generators and impacted with one another with a snap! Since there was not enough space for blades to fully form, the crystal shards collided in a blaze of light resembling a beam cannon emission but remained contained. TJ repeated the procedure several times faster and faster and each time the beams activated at the same distance. On the last time, at a subtle signal from TJ, Kain snapped his blade to life and brought it down hard on Iceman's arm. Though the hit was nicely deflected, Iceman recoiled as though his arm had been severed clean.

'It can even track multiple targets,' Buzz chuckled.

'We may have to use them with this plan of Amanda's.'

'He looks scared guys,' he smiled and put a hand on Johnny's shoulder, 'Sorry man, we probably should have brought this up in the briefing.'

'Not funny, guys! Not very funny!' Iceman said, flexing his fingers.

Twenty minutes later the rest of the group emerged in full combat readiness. The sergeants went over their respective squad's equipment and made sure the captured bolt rifles were stowed then had their own packs inspected. When everyone was checked over, Amanda gave the signal to move out. They left the bedding house in a double column formation with Buzz and Rich at the lead. The two gold Landran, assigned to watch over them, were quite adamant they could not leave but obviously they had orders not to fire on the Humans. Soon the group had a full escort of guards in a rainbow of colours as they headed towards the northeast exit of the Landran city.

One of their escorts was the Landran Commander Kraston, who urged them to rest one more day.

'You wouldn't be trying to delay us for some reason, would you?' Amanda asked, light-heartedly.

'No. No, of course not, my friend. What reason could I have to do such a thing,' he said simply.

'That's a great question,' Buzz said from the front of the formation.

'I'm just concerned that your ordeals of the past few days may be more exhausting than you realize,' Kraston almost pleaded, ignoring the junior trooper.

'Thank you for your hospitality, Kraston... perhaps we will meet again,' Amanda replied.

'Perhaps, Major Harte. Until then, if you ever need our help, you have only to ask.'

'Ask who?' TJ wondered out loud but the lizard's leader had already turned away.

As the group of Humans moved past the guard station without the escort, Kraston turned to a grey guard nearby. 'Send a unit to keep an eye on them.'

'Yes, Marshal!' replied the guard. He began to gather other greys and departed ten minutes after the Humans.

Blast, Kraston thought, one more day and the agent would have been fully trained. The job will be done though. He turned and walked back to his office, deep in thought.

The time was later in the day than they would have liked when they entered the forest. By their predictions they could make it to the edge of the sky trees by dark. Amanda was not completely sure of the way to go. Kain and Ann said they knew the way, it must be a Blademaster thing. TJ kept himself away from the decision making for most of the trek, and rarely said anything at all. His silence was uncharacteristic and Amanda was surprised how concerned she became after each passing hour.

'I think I'm seeing TJ in a similar light to the way you see him, Daniella,' Amanda said.

'Oh?' Daniella said far too quickly.

'I was trying to say that I like him a little more than I used to.'

'Ah, yeah – he's pretty neat!' she smiled although not at all relaxed.

'Ooh, girl, you got it bad,' Sam laughed.

Daniella blushed and walked away from the good-natured

banter of her friends.

'It makes no sense,' TJ said quietly.
'What doesn't?' Viper asked.
'They let us go. They put so much effort into taking us to their city and then let us walk out the next day.'
'Maybe they're tracking us. Put a locater in one of our suits.'
'No, the foreign circuit alarm would have alerted us; which means we're being followed.'
'You're paranoid, TJ! Why would they follow us?' TJ was not listening as he pulled Viper and Dolly aside.
'The rest of the troop move ahead – we'll check the rear,' he said to the formation.
'Get back in formation, Lieutenant!' Amanda ordered.
'No, Ma'am, it's my belief that we're being followed.'
'How do you know?'
'I don't know for sure, but I think it should be investigated.'
'All right, but be quick about it,' Amanda said before rejoining the convoy.

TJ led Viper and Dolly out the left side of the group and hid in the underbrush twenty feet from the path they had been following. Surprisingly, they did not have to wait long; less than a minute after the squad left, a group of six grey Landran passed almost soundlessly on either side of the path. They were divided evenly, three to each side. The three closest to TJ and the others stopped at the point at which the troopers had left the path to hide.

The reptiles aimed their rifles towards their location, sweeping back and forth so as not to travel in a straight line. Advancing as an elite combat squad, they never gave a clean shot to an enemy for long. Always two rifles covered the suspect area.

Before they got to the exact location where TJ hid, three blades flared into life. Surprised the second reptile fired a shot aimed at where Viper's head would have been, lightning reflexes and the forearm proximity blades deflected the bolt back into the lead Landran. The shot hit him in the shoulder and threw his aim off, sending his own reflex shot into the shoulder fin of TJ's suit. While the Landran was off-balance, Dolly lunged forward and pierced the torso of his target. The remaining two Landran dug in further and started to fire rapidly at the human's location.

'We can't get them out of there without some or all of us getting hurt.' Dolly pointed out.

'And we can't leave with them there.' Viper added.

'Then we get them to stay put,' TJ said looking around until he found what he needed. 'Cover me.'

The two troopers stepped up and started to deflect and dodge the barrage of rifle bolts while TJ ran to a nearby tree. A bolt slipped passed Dolly's blade and creased the armour on his side.

'Damn!' Dolly cursed, trying to recover from the hit.

Viper stepped closer to give him time. 'Hit bad?' she asked while avoiding a shot with a neat move of bracing her blade against her arm deflector.

'Nah, I'm good,' he moved up again to deflect the shots. 'What is he doing over there?'

Viper looked over to TJ for a second before a bolt caught her squarely in the chest plate. She grunted as she fell back from the impact and landed with a heavy thump.

'Viper's down, TJ, hurry up!' Dolly shouted.

TJ found the angle to the Landran he wanted, cut a wedge out of a tree and kicked it free, then sliced clean through the meter wide tree at the base of the wedge. For a moment the tree failed to move, as if the wedge was not deep enough. TJ spun around and kicked the side of the tree opposite to the wedge and started the fall. The tree fell towards the entrenched Landran and as hoped, fell directly over their position, pinning them down so they were unable to fire. Instead of congratulating himself, TJ ran towards the downed trooper. He made it to her side as Dolly helped her up. Smoke wisps rose from the tiny crater in her breastplate.

'She'll be okay, chief,' Dolly said.

'Good. If you're up to it Viper, we have to catch up to the squad.'

'I'm good to go, boss,' she smiled over a wince of pain.

'We'll get you looked at when we get to Fort Saturn,' TJ said.

'If you say so, sir,' she smiled again.

'Dolly, grab those rifles; Buzz and Kain can't be the only ones with souvenirs.'

'Yes, sir!'

While Dolly acquired the new hardware, TJ helped Viper to the path and steadied her. 'Oh, man! I lost another shoulder fin.' TJ whined partly as a joke for his injured trooper. 'If that doesn't stop, supply will stop issuing them to me!' Viper laughed.

She leaned on TJ for the couple of minutes it took Dolly to return with the rifles. Even in her armour, TJ towered a good six inches over her and she took comfort in that. His presence gave her strength. She stood on her own when Dolly returned and handed out the rifles. She tried not to look at the mark on her chest and not think about the damage that could have been done.

'So what's the plan now, Lieutenant?' Viper asked.

'Now we go back to the squad and maybe convince those other three Landran to go home.'

'We'll follow your lead, TJ,' Dolly said.

They turned up the path and ran as fast as Viper could handle and quickly closed the gap with the grey guards. The guards obviously thought the approaching steps signalled their comrades returning from the kill because they did not even bother turning around.

At TJ's direction, each of the troopers took a target and fired. The shots took the reptiles in their fans and dropped them to the forest floor. They moved up to the fallen Landran and removed their weapons. One of the three was dead and another was unconscious; the last one was stunned and was still trying to move. TJ walked up behind the crawling Landran and brought the butt of his rifle down on the back of its neck, which sent it to the land of dreams. TJ turned around in time to see Dolly fiddling with one of the reptile's packs.

'What are you doing, Ken?' asked TJ.

'I'm covering your tracks. When they miss these boys, they'll come looking for them. So, I'm going to make them think it was someone other than us,' Dolly said as he finished. 'And, I suggest we get out of here, now!'

He led TJ and the still shaken Viper quickly away from the dead and unconscious reptiles. Moments later an eerily familiar screech echoed through the trees, giving the three a spurt of energy needed to catch up to the rest of the group.

'What the hell is going on?' Amanda yelled.

'I set one of the follower's radios to its most powerful broadcast setting. That should attract the Bregan, of course,' Dolly said.

'You moron! Do you have any idea...' she started to say.

'Could we bicker someplace else, just in case they've learned how to track since we last met. Besides, Viper took a nasty hit. She'll need a scan once we've found a place to stop.'

'Okay everyone, move out. Steve, Johnny, see to Viper and make sure she can keep up,' Amanda ordered.

The eleven Humans broke into a slow jog down the path. Beyond the heavy footsteps of the formation, the forest was silent and somewhat unnerving again. Eyes constantly scanned the sides of the path for something more than the perceived invisible and imaginary threats. Small forest creatures, originally imported from Earth now almost forty years ago, scurried quietly across the path. They looked like the immigrant creatures from a distance only. Up close the mutations were evident and most were frightening.

'Something has changed these animals,' Erik said as he pried a squirrel off his suit before it could gnaw through his neck connector.

'Could be a radiation leak from the Landran ship's engine core,' Buzz said.

'Yeah, there was a lot of damage back there on that crater. And the forward engine room was nothing more than confetti,' Kain added.

'Something else we'll have to tell the Fort Saturn Commander,' Daniella said.

Rich quipped. 'Boy, I hope someone is writing this stuff down,' They spent the last two hours of their trip running away from the Landran city and around the killer anthills. It was not quite dark when they reached the edge of the forest and the valley below offered little in the way of cover. They decided to make camp inside the rim of the trees where some protection could be guaranteed. Before the light failed they had just enough time to dig themselves in and build adequate shelter.

When darkness finally came, a shift rotation for the watch was established to provide a level of security. Dolly and Rich took the first watch while the others circled around small sheltered cook fires to heat the rations and discussed plans for the next day. The only real thing accomplished was going through three igniters to start the fires. Similar to the typical bureaucracy of Old Earth, nothing was firmly decided before it was decided it was time for rest. The night in the camp passed quietly, allowed each to recuperate from some of the wear and tear of the past few days on both body and armour. A scan over Viper showed she would have a large bruise but was otherwise fine.

*****

CHAPTER XVII
Saturday, 8 April, 2251

The last watch comprised TJ and Kain. It was part of their job to decide when the rest of the group would be roused, since they would not wake on their own for several more hours. TJ decided to make another perimeter check while Kain began the process of waking the squads. His route took him eventually to the edge of the forest where he paused to admire the view.

With his back to the trees, he could see from the northeast across to the western horizon in all its unobstructed splendour. This was looking like a good day, a steady breeze had cleared away a lot of the persistent haze and the crystal dust was perfectly aligned allowing him to see considerably farther, though he still required the aide of the image enhancing equipment to pick out any details. On all sides, a grassy valley extended from the sky trees with only the occasional ripple. In the valley, there were small patches of flowers emerging in the sunlight and the occasional grove of trees. He could imagine their leaves and needles shimmering in Sol's first light like those of the sky trees. The valley floor was about two miles off, that much further from the Landran. He wished he and his people were already there.

For a moment he thought his dream had come true except he was still on the hill. He could see a digital representation of cook fires in the valley. He must be wrong! His vision enhancing equipment was not nearly good enough to pick out cook fires at almost two miles distance, even from the height advantage the hill gave him. He walked back from the edge towards the camp, trying to clear his mind of the image of the ground-bound twinkles. Given the quizzical looks those around him gave, his efforts were apparently obvious when he entered camp.

Daniella actually walked up to TJ, 'Something wrong upstairs, Lieutenant Marso?' She placed a hand gently on the biceps plating of his armour suit.

'No, I'm alright, Lieutenant Klon.' He smiled at the formality. 'Actually Daniella, if you wanted to do something to ease my mind, you could grab Sam and her cannon and bring her with you. Meet me at the edge of the trees.'

He could see a mix of confusion and disappointment in her

eyes, but that left him in more of a quandary.

'Trouble?' she asked and dropped her hand.

'No, I don't think so; I just need witnesses.' He turned and strode back to the forest's edge. Minutes after TJ reached the edge of the trees, Daniella and Sam, who was still groggy from sleep, emerged beside him. TJ spoke after a moment when it appeared Sam would fall asleep again.

'Do you two see those lights in the valley?' he pointed towards the area.

'Which... Yeah, I see them – what are they?' Daniella asked.

'Not sure, but you confirmed what I saw and now I need Sam to use her advanced targeting to ID them, if you can.'

'Already on it, Sir,' Sam yawned.

While TJ waited for Sam to report, he talked quietly to Daniella. She appeared to be enjoying herself but his mind was elsewhere, watching Sam go through a range of emotions and movements, normally not those occurring in the heavy-weapons specialist. At first her face was solemn, fully concentrating on the task, then her head snapped back in surprise. She opened her visor to rub some of the sleep from her eyes before peering back through the scope. For the second time she brought her head away from the scope, though only an inch or two this time and briefly shook it. Once again she looked into the eyepiece, this time she smiled, starting to laugh softly.

'What's the word, sergeant?' Daniella asked.

'The word, Ma'am,' she giggled, 'is that TJ... sorry, Lieutenant Marso was right; they are cook fires, the air is rippling and magnifying a little but I can make it out clearly.'

'Okay, and so who's doing the cooking?' TJ asked.

'I don't recognize them but then, even at maximum zoom, I can't tell too many details. What I do know is that there are six sleds and I counted twenty-three armoured personnel in the camp. I could barely make out the unit insignia on the closest vehicle as belonging to a Fort Grey sled.' Her voice rose excitedly as she reported.

'Do you know what that means, TJ? It has to be Commander Martel's refugees!' Daniella replied, but TJ was gone. She spun around in time to see the sparse foliage of the sky trees closing behind him. 'Come on, Sam!' and she bolted back towards camp with the trooper in tow.

TJ burst into the camp's small clearing followed closely by

Daniella and Sam. His abrupt entrance made everyone jump to their feet with blades at the ready although not activated.

'We have contact in the valley,' he announced. 'Most likely it's a refugee caravan from Fort Grey.' The group burst into a spontaneous cheer. 'We'll have to leave now if we're going to catch them. With your permission, of course, Major.'

Amanda stepped forward, 'You heard the Lieutenant. Let's go!' She gave TJ a subtle smile for the show of respect.

'Why you being so nice to her all of a sudden?' Buzz asked.

'I don't know who's going to see the next sunrise, Bill. When I'm sure , and that day comes, then we can have fun again. Deal?'

'Deal, chief.'

'Spread the word. I want the First Recon to feel like they're a part of us. Not the other way around, mind you.'

'Yes, sir!' He saluted and set about getting ready.

Minutes after the command was given to ready the squads, the first trooper emerged from the edge of the sky trees and began the descent into the valley. The eleven Humans took up a wide spread, seemingly scattered formation as soon as they cleared the forest as if they were readying for combat. The three officers also disbursed through the formation, TJ on point, Daniella, rear guard.

The lights in the valley were gone by the time they started out and without them it was impossible to locate the Fort Grey convoy, even in the full light of Sol. The squad moved on in a northerly direction and hoped they would see the convoy or alternatively they would see them. They moved at a slightly accelerated pace because of the decline of the slope leading away from the Highland Plateau. It took them an hour to reach the valley floor and they marched another two hours before they stopped for lunch. Amanda kept the break short before she moved them out quickly in fear they might miss the convoy.

After yet another uneventful tour of the terrain, the squad found themselves in a lower part of the valley with almost no view of the west or east. TJ prompted the squad to pause there while he sent Buzz and Dolly up the eastern side to see if they could locate the convoy. Buzz managed the climb better than the older Dolly and achieved the micro-summit ahead of him. Fortunately, that gave him enough time to jump out of the way of the GCR cresting the hill at the same moment. He rolled away from the underside of the vehicle before it settled to an idle hover.

'Holy crap, bud, you okay?' said the driver as he jumped out of the sled.

'Found them!' Buzz hollered when he had finished rolling.

Dolly stood mere inches from the nose of this lead sled and said in a quiet monotone, 'Thanks Buzz. I never would have guessed.'

'Damn those things are quiet,' he grunted. Buzz nodded his head once he had struggled to his feet and dusted off his armour in the process, he swept away some caked-on mud previously covering his insignia.

'By the light! You're Fort Grey's!' the driver looked down the hill towards the advancing squad, then turned back towards the second sled. 'Commander Martel, it's Major Harte's squads!' he shouted. The excited guard quickly spun back around and saluted the Major.

'At ease, Corporal,' Amanda said returning his salute. 'I need to speak with Commander Martel immediately.'

'Yes, Major!'

'TJ, Daniella set up camp here so we can all get some rest before we start for Fort Saturn tomorrow.'

'But, Major, there's four hours of travel time left. We could get to Fort Saturn in two if we push on now,' TJ said.

'You heard, Lieutenant – now do it!' she ordered.

'Yes, Ma'am' he replied with a hint of resentment.

TJ began giving orders for a camp to be established in the depression within the larger valley. Fire shelters and sleeping covers were built while the six sleds circled the makeshift compound, two technicians were assigned to set up a maintenance tent and begin refitting all the new suits with the forearm shields. A third tech-trained trooper was tasked with recharging all the power modules in the suits and replacing the power cells in the blades. The lone researcher from Martel's squad also began a thorough study of one of the Recon bolt rifles. Both groups filled each other in on the happenings, telling stories well into the night about their earlier adventures.

*****

It was two hours after the setting of Bane when TJ gathered a some troopers and himself, outside the firelight. He had originally planned this expedition for four troopers and himself, somehow Erik had found out about the plan and demanded to be included.

'You're not coming, Erik, you don't have enough training for this,' TJ had said.

'Look, Lieutenant, I know I'm a still green but you've got to take me, you'll probably need the manpower! Besides, you said it yourself; it's a routine advance scout. It's just a diplomatic jaunt, anyway.'

'That's what this whole journey has been about from the start and look what's happened so far. No! You have to stay.'

'How am I supposed to become experienced if I can't get any experience?' Erik smiled, knowing he had trumped any further argument TJ could offer. Now he stood proudly as the other four troopers stepped up. First to arrive was Johnny with a new cannon, followed closely by the intimidating Kain. The last two arrived at the same time, with Buzz practically hitting on a smiling Ashley. That was all but one of the remains of the Second Recon, Fort Grey division.

'Unfortunately, Dolly has to stay here to finish the refit of the armour but he knows the plan. We are going on a simple recon of Fort Saturn – we've had too many surprises on this trip already. I'll drive out while you five get as much rest as possible, then Buzz will take us home. We don't have official approval but Dolly knows how to handle the Brass.'

'Which gopher are we taking, chief?' Buzz asked.

'Everyone load into the larger sled as discreetly as possible. It's an assault sled.'

'Good, that will be a little more elbow room,' he smiled.

They split up and moved back into the light of the fire to socialize with the troopers that remained awake. Half an hour later they had slowly regrouped inside the assault sled. TJ was the last to enter and slid behind the controls. He turned around in his chair and gave the thumbs up sign, returned by the five troopers in the back.

'Here we go,' he whispered to himself and engaged the engine.

The firing up of the reactor drew a couple of casual glances but no action. GCRs have had their reactors turned on and off at various times since they had made camp, for systems checks. But when the sled slipped off into the night the camp exploded in panic with the watch trying to stop the sled and the officers trying to figure out what happened. Amanda was going to order a sled to go after it when the Commander, who had been talking to Dolly, stopped her.

'Major, could you come here for a moment, please?' Martel said while waving her over.

'Yes, sir,' she said stepping closer. 'I was just about to order a pursuit.'

'That won't be necessary Amanda. Ken was just telling me TJ's plan and, under the circumstances, I agree with it.'

'TJ did this? What plan?' She was furious.

'They're all traitors!' Ann yelled above the racket.

'He and a small group have gone ahead to Fort Saturn to ensure a clear path and deliver a message, if possible.' Martel said without looking at the Blademaster.

'That's insane! I would never have let him go.'

'Neither would I and that's why he went – because he knew we'd say no. But now that I've had a moment to think about it, it's a good idea, regardless of my feelings.'

'There will be Hell to pay when and if he gets back!'

'Let's hope it's when, eh?' He left a fuming Amanda Harte and retired to his sleep.

'Her head's probably spinning right now,' Buzz laughed.

The entire group was laughing at Buzz's estimation of the events back at the camp. Even TJ wore a smile because he could almost picture Amanda's head twirling on her shoulders.

'Okay everyone, settle down and get some rest. If the past is intent on repeating itself then we're going to see some action before we get there,' TJ announced.

'And we are sure to see some when we get back,' Erik joked.

Everyone laughed again at whatever mental pictures sprang up, before slowly drifting off to a peaceful sleep to dream of their CO and the Major battling it out yet again. TJ eased the velocity of the sled up to its maximum governed speed and sped through the night towards Fort Saturn.

Three hours after the Second Recon went on their renegade mission; the fourth watch was on duty and walking the perimeter. The watch was made up of four troopers, each a quarter of the way along the circular patrol pattern. On one of his rounds along the western ridge of the micro valley in which the camp was made, the guard noticed a glint of firelight coming from a dark shape a hundred yards from his location. He unhooked his blade and moved in a south-westerly direction towards the shadow.

When he got to a range of twenty yards, he noticed the shadow move and heard whispering. The movement of the shadow uncovered more of its angles revealed in the moonlight. The pattern that was forming was of a suit of armour hunched over something. At eight yards away, the guard stopped – something was not right here! The person in the suit was talking to the *something* it huddled over and made no indication it acknowledged the presence of the guard.

'What are you doing out here, pal?' the guard asked.

'Go away, Human!' the shadow armour said with a distinct hiss in its voice that may or may not have been static.

The guard's blade erupted into blinding light and the guard set himself for a fight. 'Identify yourself or surrender your weapons!' he shouted.

The shadow spun to face the guard with a low rumbling growl emanating from its armour speakers. Light glinted off an instrument in the shadowed hands, bringing confusion to the guard. Confusion was quickly replaced with recognition – and with recognition came fear. With the guard's fear came an emerald green bolt from the shadow's instrument. The bolt slammed into the weakest part of the guard's armour, the visor. The hit did not kill the guard, merely stunned him and sent him sprawling to the ground.

The guard struggled to get to his blade laying a couple of yards away but instead found himself at the boot of the shadow. Looming over the helpless guard, the shadowed armour directed the bolt rifle at his head and fired without saying a word. The guard's empty helmet bounced off the ground with the shattered visor staring towards the dim lights of the Human camp. By the movement across the lights, the guard next in the patrol was silhouetted but continued the patrol pattern without noticing his missing comrade.

'Rise and shine, sleepy heads,' TJ called back from the front seat of the now-parked sled.

'Where are we, chief?' Buzz asked yawning.

'Four and half miles out of Fort Saturn. We're in a crater field to the east of the fort.'

'All right! Gear up and outside in ten!' Iceman hollered.

Like so many times before, TJ was the first out of the sled since he had not been sleeping, scanning the area.

Buzz was next and joined in the effort to secure the *dent* they currently called home. A couple of moments later the other four had piled out of the assault sled and formed up in front of TJ.

'Okay, now, listen up!' TJ whispered loud enough to be heard but no louder. He did not want to use the short range comm. on the off chance someone or something might hear them. 'I can't see Fort Saturn from here, so we'll assume that they are under Alert-Two conditions. We're just going to see if the way is clear. No contact!'

'Yes, sir,' the group echoed.

'Let's go. Viper, you've got the point.'

The unit moved ahead in a hex formation and, with the assistance of the power armour, managed to run at a half-crouch. They moved in this fashion for an hour before stopping to scout Fort Saturn at the three quarter-mile range mark. TJ gestured to signal silence and for Iceman to join him in the lead observer position.

TJ whispered, 'Tell me what you see, Iceman.'.

'There's a lot of movement, boss. Looks like the Fort is in at least Alert-Three,' he said, looking through his cannon's scope.

'There shouldn't be as many people outside at condition Three.'

Iceman solemnly looked up from his scope. 'They aren't people, TJ. They're Bregan and they're mad by the looks of things.'

'Bregan... damn.' TJ looked back to the other four troopers crouched behind some shrubs, 'We're leaving, Ice.'

'We're gone. Roger that!'

The two of them slipped back to the others and directed them to make a hasty retreat. They made the best time they could back to their sled – a forty-five minute trip instead of an hour. After they reached the GCR, TJ ordered three of the troopers to join him in a defensive position while Buzz fired up the engines and Ashley readied the cannon.

'I don't think we were followed but keep your eyes open,' TJ told them.

The sound of the engines coming to life brought relief to the troopers but the drawn-out echo of screeches that followed brought terror. Instantly the troopers began to look for their adversaries. The dark of the night seemed to get heavier as the seconds ticked by.

The indentation which worked well to hide them severely limited their vision out. The arrival of the Bregan into combat was announced by Ashley's shot from the beam cannon. The brilliant blue beam only dimly lit the night but nicely pinpointed the target and the seven others around it. Before the light faded the targeted Bregan could be seen crumpling beneath its comrades.

'We're steaming. Let's go, people!' Buzz shouted from the control seat.

As if the announcement was a trigger for the fighting to begin, dozens of eyes in the dark came to life. Moments later, the eerie glow and pulse of their wings turned night into day. Forearm scythes ignited in anticipation of combat and more than a few blades added their light.

'You heard the man – let's go!' TJ ordered.

The sled's cannon let off a couple more shots, darkening some eyes and wings forever. The four troopers edged back to the sled but were attacked mere fifteen feet from the door. Ten Bregan descended upon them from the green haze, quickly down to nine thanks to Iceman's cannon. Two more fell to TJ and Kain's whirling blades while a third one had a fight going with Erik.

'Come on! Last one in is going to be a Bregan playmate.' Kain jibed before he dove into the sled.

A green beam cut past the door behind Kain and sliced a perfect line through a Bregan warrior. TJ felled another one before he tossed a flash ball near the two Bregan Erik was now fighting. The ball went off on impact, rattling one Bregan off the side of the sled and the other bowled into four others trying to enter the fight. TJ grabbed the loading handle on Erik's pack on his way to the sled door.

'Quit playing around, Iceman, you can pick it up tomorrow.' TJ shouted.

TJ was climbing into the sled with Erik right behind as the sled shuddered from the release of another beam. Simultaneously, Johnny's beam went through two more Bregan who were recovering from the impact of their fellow attacker.

'Coming, Mother,' Iceman cried out.

Turning from the now numerous potential targets, he ran to the sled. TJ was in the process of helping Erik in, when he saw two of the last Bregan in mismatched power armour attack Johnny. The first swipe took out his cannon while the second hit glanced off his pack. Using his lightning quick reflexes, Iceman snapped on his blade and brought it to the side of the head of the second attacker. Unfortunately, his spin allowed the first to impale him with its stolen blade. The blade ruptured the reactor, which caused a twirling fireball. The blast incinerated both the human and the Bregan while the shockwave smashed into Erik's back and sent him crashing into the sled.

'By the Light!' Ashley said hoarsely.

'Go! Go! Go!' Kain shouted.

The GCR shot forward, knocking several of the gargoyles over, while Kain and TJ tended to an unconscious Erik. Whimpers of loss could be heard from the gunner chair above the almost continuous hum of the beam cannon.

'Viper, knock it off! We need the power to get out of here,' Buzz said as compassionately as possible.

The GCR doubled its forward speed when Viper stopped her attempt at revenge. Slipping out of the seat, she knelt beside Erik.

'You two get some sleep. I'll watch him,' she said.

'You sure, Ashley?' TJ asked.

'Yeah, I'm fine. I need this, TJ, please!' She was almost in tears again.

'Okay, Viper. Try to rest anyway,' he said, putting a hand on her shoulder.

'Thanks.'

'Camp in two, everyone,' Buzz announced.

The sled remained silent both inside and out for the rest of the trip. No one stirred more than they had to, but little rest was had.

The GCR emerged into the fire light, still two hours before the rise of Sol. It was battered; deep gashes crisscrossed its armour plating and it had a noticeable indentation on the right side. The early rising troopers gathered around the beat-up vehicle and stared almost in awe when living people emerged. The medics instantly took Erik to the medical tent while the techs slowly approached the sled, dread at the thought of trying to fix it.

While the techs were inspecting the damage, the Commander and Major emerged from their respective tents to see why the entire camp was now awake. When their eyes settled on the scarred GCR and the four troopers standing outside, the Commander shook his head. He knew by the look in TJ's eyes, another trooper was down. Amanda, on the other hand, went ballistic.

'What the hell was going through your mind/' she bellowed.

'I thought...' TJ started to explain.

'The hell you did! You broke so many regulations with your little journey that I don't know where to start!'

'You're doing fine,' Kain said quietly.

'Stow it, Sergeant,' she ordered, 'and where's Mr. Gentry? He should hear this, too. I don't want to repeat myself.'

'He's dead, Major,' Viper whispered.

'I... Oh dear, I'm sorry,' she said quietly, 'but that is an excellent reason why you shouldn't have gone out. TJ, you're responsible for the loss of Johnny. I expect you to surrender your blade when we reach Fort Saturn.'

'He'll do no such thing, Major,' Commander Martel cut in, 'until we determine if negligence or misconduct was a party to Sergeant Gentry's death.'

'Yes, sir!'

'What happened out there, Lieutenant?' Commander Martel asked.

'As you know from Dolly, er... Corporal Michelson, we six went on an advance scout of Fort Saturn. With the amount of conflict we've had in the last week and a half, I decided it was a prudent course of action. During our recon we discovered Fort Saturn was either under siege or is about to be. Bregan followed us back to the sled where they attacked. Sergeant Gentry died defending the sled so that the warning could make it back here.'

'Do you all agree with what Lieutenant Marso just said?' Martel asked.

'Yes, sir. That's the way it went down.' Buzz replied.

'Of course they'll agree. He's their CO and friend,' Amanda stated.

'What would you have me do, Major? The entire unit has the same story. Would you like me to launch an investigation when all that it will prove is you have some kind of grudge against one of our best officers? You'd better heed my words, Major Harte. If you continue this course of action, you'll find yourself in a heap of trouble!'

'Yes, sir. Sorry, sir.'

'TJ lost one of his men so that the rest of us don't get wasted today,' Daniella added, joining the conversation.

'I'm sorry about Johnny, TJ,' Amanda said before she went back to her tent.

'Sir, it was just a recon. I hadn't planned on engaging the enemy,' TJ said once Amanda's presence was gone.

'I know, Lieutenant, and it works out for the greater good in the long run. Now we can get the drop on them. Anyhow, you four get an hour's rest or so. I'll check on your Private. The rest of the squads will ready the convoy before we set out.'

'Thank you, Commander,' TJ said, leading his people to a quieter corner of the camp.

*****

CHAPTER XVIII
Monday, 9 April, 2251

The sky above the Eden Peninsula lightened the near pitch black of night serenely to navy blue-green then to an almost powder blue, sea-foam colour before erupting into fiery red and orange –the heavens announcing the rebirth of Sol for the day. Many of the thirty-four Humans moving north towards Fort Saturn, both on foot or in one of the six sleds, looked to the east and silently asked Sol for her protection and blessing. It was the first Human offensive in what some were silently calling the Last Terran War. Officially there was no declaration but then, most of the Human race knew nothing of the threat they faced.

The convoy moved along at a steady pace with an estimated time of arrival at Fort Saturn of two more hours at this point. The fifth sled in formation was the assault sled that had made this journey the night before. Because of the damage it was no longer capable of long-term combat and had been converted into an armed medical vehicle. While it was unfortunate one of the sleds was lost, in terms of combat potential, at the same time it was good to have a field medic post to care for the injured. Presently, the medic on board was in the final stages of healing the still-groggy Erik Krushell.

The plan of attack had been discussed with everyone so they all would know what to do. This kept the talking to a minimum although the rookies of the group whispered between themselves. Occasionally a blade would be flared into life in an effort to double check its readiness and relieve tension. A unit of four troopers was given the Landran bolt rifles and assigned to protect Sam, the sole remaining heavy-weapons specialist. The trooper on point was equipped with a long distance sensor suit to scan for any sign of Bregan movement. Eyes of most of the walking troopers were almost always locked on him, waiting for his signal.

'I've counted twice, Commander, but we are still one short,' Daniella said.

'Then that helmet we found must have belonged to the missing trooper. Who was on watch with him?' Martel asked.

'The schedule sheet got messed up pretty badly but from what I can determine the only missing name was on Ann Huston's shift.

Members from the fifth watch reported relieving Ann. One said he asked her where their fourth man was and she replied he just walked off into the night.'

'Obviously that can't be right since we found the helmet less than a hundred yards from the patrol route. She should have been able to see something.'

'Unless she was the one doing in the poor fellow,' TJ added.

'What are you suggesting, Lieutenant? That one of our Blademaster is a turncoat?' Martel asked, shocked.

'She's always been hostile towards me but after we left the Landran city and did in those grey-scaled fellows she really didn't like me.'

'That's just your imagination,' Daniella replied, waving a dismissive hand.

'Is it? I was thinking about the recon last night and there is no way those Bregan could have followed without our knowing. Their primary mode of travel is flight. On the ground I doubt that there would be any way they could keep up and in flight their wings glow. Don't you see, we would have seen them flying after us. They had to have been waiting for us. Someone let them know we were coming and a spy in our ranks makes sense.'

'Okay, it does make sense when you stop to think. Daniella, pass an order change on to Ann that she is now guarding the medical sled. Send Kain to take her place to guard Major Harte. And send the major to me.'

'Yes, sir.' She saluted.

TJ walked over to Buzz before Amanda got to Commander Martel's side. He could see anger in her eyes as she stared at him until Martel began to relay the information he had so far. Her eyes glazed and her face went pale as she came to the same conclusion.

'What's up, Chief,' Buzz repeated, when TJ hadn't answered for the second time. He punctuated his third with a shot to his arm.

'Hey!' TJ jerked back.

'For the fourth time, what's going on?'

'You have to keep this secret, okay?'

'Sure, no problem.'

'Okay, the deal is that there is most likely...' TJ started.

'A mole, spy whatever, right?' Buzz cut in.

'Ah, yeah. How did you know?' asked a slightly puzzled TJ. Buzz was smart, this he knew, but that leap was a bit much even for him.

'Kain, Viper and I were talking about it before we left and we decided we were set up.'

'That's what I figured as well. We also think we know who it is but we'll have to wait, it seems.'

They walked on in silence for an hour and a quarter before the point man gave the signal. The combat-ready GCRs swung into the abreast formation and twelve of the twenty walking troopers took their place amongst them. The remaining eight infantry crouched next to the medical sled and waited for the signal for their entry into the fray. The fire team, including Sam and the four riflemen, would go in first and set up a defensives line.

Sam and her unit started forward at the signal from Daniella and shortly took their position on a small hill providing them with a perfect view of the two-mile battlefield. Even though the last half of the field ahead was sheltered by the atmospheric haze, the fire team's image enhancing equipment compensated well.

When they crested the hill they were greeted with a sight no one ever thought would come to Eden. In the distance was Fort Saturn, a massive complex and city within two rings of walls and turrets. Behind, though twenty miles off, was the top of the impressive wall of the Comb Plateau, rising almost a mile into the air. That image of the city was the classic view of travel brochures back in the Terran days, though the turrets were not built at the time. Impressive as it was, the view of the fortress now before them was certainly unforgettable.

Surrounding the mighty Fort were countless hundreds of Bregan, swarming to and from the wall. Fiery red beams of the class-7 beam cannons pulsed away from the turrets on the inner wall combining their light with the fabulous blue of the class-5 beam cannons on the outer wall. Half a dozen Bregan fell with each flash but were quickly replaced by a dozen more. Two breaches in the wall could be seen from the hill and the smoke inside the outer wall, meaning Bregan were inside. Fort Saturn was about to fall.

'Set yourselves, boys, this is going to get nasty,' Sam ordered. She raised her hand, a signal her unit was ready, and braced herself for a quick and unpleasant response to the next action. Even before she was ready, the second domino fell.

From a field radio set to three mile range, came the voice of Lieutenant Trevor James Marso of the First Recon, Fort Grey division.

'Message for District Commander Shawn Norris of Fort Saturn. This is Lieutenant TJ Marso, Second Recon, Fort Grey, plus two. We stand ready to assist you.'

The message was broadcast over open frequency, naturally drawing the attention of nearly all the Bregan. The screech was certainly deafening but the response from Fort Saturn made it through somehow.

'... This is Fort Saturn, the sun is setting. Your assistance would be appreciated, Fort Grey.'

That official response for a life-threatening emergency had a devastating effect on the troopers and it was also the trigger for the wave of Fort Grey infantry and vehicles to surge forward. Their hearts swelled with pride at the mention of their former base and the thought of preventing the loss of another Terran fort fuelled their aggression.

'For the Grey!' they shouted, commencing their charge.

The two transmissions coming from two directions aggravated the Bregan to the point of confusion. This halt in their actions no doubt ended many of them, especially inside the outer wall. It also provided the beams with multiple unmoving targets.

The fire team opened fire seconds before the five sleds and eight infantry surged over the hill. Sam's beam cannon had been field modified by Dolly for rapid fire if she needed it, a modification taken from the Landran bolt rifle. Unsure about the reliability of the new technology, Sam chose to use the standard beam mode.

The first beam shot and the first two rifle bolts caught the Bregan completely off guard and stopped nine halfway through their attack. The Bregan recoiled from the Fort Grey division as it charged over the hill; some even started flying away when the beam cannons from the GCRs started to fire. A dozen more fell before they began to regroup.

'Fort Saturn, continue to transmit. The dual signal is confusing them,' Amanda announced on a second field radio.

'Roger, Fort Grey. Will comply.'

Both sides left their units on transmit while they fought. Many of the Bregan began to leave for any point east and away from the signals. The closer creatures fought harder, as if they wanted to smash the source of the transmissions. Blade combat intensified while the cannons and rifles continued to blaze.

'Second group advance to support the fire positions,' Commander Martel ordered.

The eight troopers plus Erik, his medic and the sled all but jumped onto the hill next to Sam. The reinforcements came a few seconds before a squad of Bregan separated from the main group and charged the hill. Simultaneously, the swarm seemed to swallow the advancing Humans. Focused on the role of cover fire for the sleds and footmen, the fire team did not see the convoy heading for them. The first and last of the charging squad of Bregan were blasted out of existence by the medic-sled's cannon while the rest engaged one-on-one with the second group.

Sam switched her cannon to pulse mode and opened fire. The resulting effect stunned almost everyone on both sides. Bolts the size of Sam's armoured forearm began flying out of her weapon with the same impact power as an actual beam shot. Though less accurate, in terms of killing power, the bolts hit a remarkable number of times. Bregan with arm, leg, and non-fatal torso wounds fell at an astounding rate.

Large numbers of Bregan made a hasty retreat. Those remaining staying witnessed the pulse cannon quickly overheat to the point where Sam had to discard the weapon. The damage to the cannon was done and the core went critical. The leeway to detonation allowed Sam enough time to toss the doomed weapon down the hill into a slowly advancing pack of Bregan. The explosion wave pulverized the pack and even knocked the fire group down.

'Let's get messy, fellas!' Sam said, activating her blade before she got up.

The second group opened a corridor to the first group who were down by at least one GCR, though the occupants seemed to have made it out of the shredded vehicle without injury. In a matter of minutes ninety percent of the initial Humans outside Fort Saturn remained and were regrouped again. Around them was a field of dead and dying Bregan and a few Humans who would never see the beauty of Sol again.

'What are you doing here, Sergeant Cornwall?' Daniella asked, effortlessly turning aside a Bregan's attack.

'Gun blew up, lieutenant,' Sam replied and blocked an attacking swing before spinning around to attack, only to have her efforts stopped short of the target by the Bregan's forearm scythe.

'Shame about that,' Daniella commented as she finally got under the Bregan's defence and struck home.

'Yes, ma'am.'

There was a pause in the action as the Bregan, whose numbers were greatly diminished, tried to figure out a way to smash the two formations of the Humans. With the dual transmissions beating down on them, the process took longer than one might have expected. The pause allowed the field medic from the first group to pull Viper away from the battle line to try to patch her up.

'Thanks for the cover, bud,' she said to the armoured man who had stepped in front of her after she went down.

'No problem,' Dolly smiled over his shoulder.

'Should have known you'd pull something macho like that when you got the chance,' she laughed.

'You know me.'

'Please, lay still, Corporal,' the medic said while examining her wound.

TJ leaned over to Martel while he kept an eye on the front line of Bregan. 'You do pretty good, old man, for a pacifist.'

'Just because I don't like fighting doesn't mean I can't, sonny.'

'Boss, I think we're in trouble.' Buzz interjected.

'What makes you think that, Buzz?' TJ asked focusing harder on the front line of the enemy force.

'Well, I'm not entirely sure but the way they're all backing up is a little unnerving. I don't think it has anything to do with the cannons.'

For the first time, TJ noticed the fire team and the five remaining sleds were still firing despite the Bregan's lack of action.

'Hold your fire! Hold your fire!' TJ shouted waving his off hand into the air.

The cannons and rifles stopped their attack and silence descended on the field of battle. The Bregan continued their slow retreat until two hundred yards from the Human ring. There they stopped and settled in.

'I don't know what you people are doing out there but those creatures have withdrawn from the outer ring. Our observers have reported three-quarters of them have flown the coop.' Fort Saturn's commander transmitted.

'We didn't do a whole lot, sir,' Amanda replied from the field radio she had dropped earlier.

'Well, keep it up, my dear.' Commander Norris chuckled.

The two groups of combatants sized each other up until well after midday. The one side was vibrating with tension. It was like a dam moments before bursting. The other side tried to keep its own tension in check. The respite gave the medics enough time to move two seriously injured troopers into the medi-sled and the techs sufficient time to remove any functional components from the damaged sled and relocate them to another vehicle. Many of the troopers knelt or squatted while they talked quietly amongst themselves waiting for the next onslaught.

'Maybe they have casualty limits like we do,' Buzz suggested.

'Or they may have just morale issues,' Kain quipped.

laughing at their joke, the mirth spread through the formation. It was never really funny but they all needed a tension reliever.

'Let's try moving towards Fort Saturn, everyone,' Martel suggested.

'Just for shits and giggles, eh?' Kain smiled.

'You got it,' Martel returned his smile.

They started to move as a unit within seconds of each other. Pilots of the sleds jumped into their crafts and the troopers bolted to their feet without complaint. The troopers, who had turned off their blades in that first hour of calm, brought them back to life. The Bregan wall around them shifted with them, always keeping the same distance... until the last trooper cleared the ring of the dead Bregan, then all hell broke loose! Half the creatures soared into the air above the Humans while the other half closed the gap like a bear trap. They swarmed so thickly it seemed to the group of Humans they were in a cocoon made completely of Bregan with scythes, winds and glowing eye providing the light. Then the flying Bregan turned off their wings and descended.

The first attack came against TJ who somehow got in the perfect hit on his descending aggressor to knock it, unhurt, away from him. Amanda was extending her blade to deflect the attack against TJ when the Bregan impaled itself in its efforts to compensate for the earlier hit. Quick thinking and reflexes on Amanda's part prevented the large creature from knocking her down. When the body reached the hilt of the blade, Amanda rotated her shoulder as she would have for a hip toss and threw the limp form into the oncoming wave of Bregan. She was stunned for a second at the remarkable feat, missing the incoming attack of a large grey Bregan.

The big grey brought its blade down on Amanda's weapon,

knocking it out of the way, then gave her a forearm chop across the chest with its scythe. That sent her flying into the middle of the circle. The big grey then went on a rampage through the Human ranks.

Kain found himself separated from the formation, how he could not say. For the moment he was alone with no Bregan to engage. He used this opportunity to study the surrounding conflict, as he was accustomed to doing. A blue beam crossed the sky overhead and the occasional green bolt zipped past only to take a piece out of one of the Bregan, Kain was watching. A peculiar sight caught his full attention despite one of the GCRs turning into a massive fireball. It was the image of a large grey Bregan near the centre of the Human formation, swinging its arms and blade madly and occasionally actually picking up a trooper in full armour and tossing him or her into the crowd of waiting Bregan where the unfortunate soul was quickly cut to shreds and probably devoured.

Kain's bystander status was shattered when a torso, with an armoured arm the only thing still attached, landed at his feet. The feeding crowd spun around to follow the course of the body fragment and was shocked to see another Human standing over their snack. Kain seized the moment to slowly bend down and take the blade from the armoured hand, then rose to his full height, roughly six inches above the creatures around him.

The Bregan's eyes flared a split second before the Human Blademaster activated his second blade. Then, like the quarterback in a football game, he was rushed from all sides.

'Ours is not to wonder why,' he muttered as he called on all his training and experience to keep himself from becoming gargoyle fodder, or something like that.

He waited until the last possible moment before leaping into the air. With the aid of his power armour he was able to clear their heads by a foot. Until now, the Humans who had fought the Bregan had always stayed on the ground, which meant these creatures were ill-prepared for this aerial manoeuvre and the ring collapsed into a pile beneath the airborne trooper. While in the air, a blast from one of the sleds impacted Kain's proximity shield on his left forearm. The beam split into two with one half cutting down two Bregan in the distance while the other split cut a line across Kain's visor before hitting a flying adversary that had approached undetected.

While the shot did not kill the creature, it knocked it from the sky. The crippled Bregan bowled its way into the crowd and cleared a spot for Kain to land.

On his way down, he brought his two blades down on two Bregan heading up to get him. One caught the blade in the head and was dead before it hit the ground, while the other took the hit through the shoulder and wing, crippling them both. It fell to the ground awkwardly.

Once on the ground, Kain put his fighting skills to the test. They came at him as best they could, sometimes as many as six at once. They would come at him and he bested them one after another by parrying or blocking their attacks, then punching, kicking, stabbing or cutting them down.

A bold creature dove at the Blademaster who did a flying somersault over the assailant and landed in a tuck-and-roll. During the roll, he released a flash ball behind him. He came out of his roll in the thrust position with his blade in under the arm of a grey Bregan and his second blade sweeping through another creature that happened to get too close.

The flash ball went off and cleared a sixteen-foot circle next to the remaining Humans. The Bregan at the edge of the clearing were in a jumble of arms, legs and wings. Kain withdrew his blade from the small grey Bregan's head, letting it crumple to the ground. He did a reverse tumble ending in a forward somersault allowing him to throw his second blade into the clearing and the pack of Humans.

TJ had seen the large grey Bregan tear apart some of his troopers and even knock down Amanda and now it was time to show him the true meaning of pain. He caught up to the big creature as it bore down on Daniella, who had her hands full already, and ignoring all the other threats, proceeded to plant his armoured boot into the small of its back. TJ was almost mauled by the smaller brown Bregan when the big grey on the turf bellowed over the hum of many blades.

'That one's mine!' it yelled, getting to its feet.

TJ looked around and noticed, other than a couple of one-on-one fights and a small skirmish in the distance, both sides had stopped their fighting to look on the fight at the heart of the conflict. Bregan and Human stood, or squatted, seemingly side-by-side, although the enemies remained out of reach.

'Let's see if the Human can fight face-to-face,' Big Grey

snarled.

'You can't fight me, Bregan,' TJ smiled 'You're only able to strike the weak or unsuspecting.'

The Bregan took a step forward, its scythes flaring and the blade in its massive hand hummed its tune of destruction. Then TJ ran head long into the duel, with his blade humming along and most of his armour shimmering in the fading daylight.

The two converged in a frightening display of whirling energy. Blades met with angry snaps and plasma flares of disintegrating crystals. Forearm scythes viciously slashed the air only to be stopped by a blade or forearm shield.

Despite his eager entrance into this combat, TJ found himself outmatched and was forced to fall back to avoid being diced. Hits were scored by both combatants though none serious but there were more against TJ. When the two paused after a couple of minutes, for Big Grey to catch his breath, TJ finally got to survey the damage to his armour. Scratches and cuts, some deep, adorned every section of the armour. He could read about the breaches being reported to him on his heads-up display.

TJ knew he could not defend himself forever this way and a change of action was called for. Without waiting for Big Grey to get set for the next round, he charged in to assault again. The Bregan had been expecting the charge but still had trouble holding his ground.

The blows came fast and furious. TJ was using everything he had to win this round because the next round would not see him come out victorious. With kicks, punches and a twirling blade, TJ regained most of the ground he had lost earlier.

The Bregan's defence faltered as a blade spun from out of the crowd, piercing the creature's flank. TJ wasted no time in executing a series of moves, knocked the Bregan's defences aside before he cleanly placed his blade at the heart of the beast.

As Big Grey fell, cheers erupted from the Humans and a screech echoed from the hundred and fifty Bregan. The Bregan, seeing the blade fly from the crowd, followed TJ's gaze towards a lone human Blademaster slowly getting to his feet. His eyes locked on to Kain in appreciation, totally oblivious to the surrounding chaos.

The Bregan tried to start the fight up again but found they were too close to the Humans to get a good attack started.

The Humans' blades ripped through the air before the Bregan

knew what hit them. Beams sang from the vehicles in every direction while the bolt rifles fired over and over.

Nearly a third of the Bregan forces were cut down in one way or another before they could organize a full retreat. In a matter of minutes the battlefield was clear of any living Bregan and cheers rang out from both of the Human camps.

'Thanks for the assist, Paul,' TJ saluted.

'No problem, lieutenant.' Kain smiled, returning his salute. 'I didn't think I'd hit anything with it.' He reached down and removed the blade from the side of the dead Bregan and picked up its ill-gotten blade as well.

'He won't be needing this, I don't think.' Kain said handing the dead Bregan's weapon to TJ, 'You earned this, TJ.'

'Thanks.'

'TJ!' Dolly yelled, 'You'd better get over here.'

TJ rushed over to where Dolly was standing. In front of them, two medics were feverishly working on a fallen trooper.

'Who it is?' TJ asked.

'It's the Major, sir.'

'Damn!' TJ knelt beside his wounded commanding officer.

'Hey there, fella,' Amanda said from behind an oxygen mask. 'Heard you won, back there.'

'Yeah, I had some help. You just get better, okay?'

'I'm trying, but I'm so tired.'

'We have to get her to the fort now, sir.' said one of the medics, gently pushing the lieutenant aside.

'I'll see you at Saturn, Amanda. Get some rest.'

'She doesn't look good, TJ,' Dolly said.

'I know,' he said to Dolly. Then to a passing medic, 'Let me know directly when her condition changes.'

'Yes, sir.'

The medical GCR was pulling away when Daniella walked up with Steve Gallagher in tow. Her head hung low and it looked as if she might start crying at any moment.

'They got Rich, too.'

'I'm sorry, Dani,' TJ said, hugging her.

He knew it was hard on her to lose a squad member, especially after she had lost her entire first squad. It was always hard to lose a Blademaster like Rich Jones, no matter the circumstances.

'Preliminary counts are in, folks,' Commander Martel said

grimly, 'We have six wounded and seventeen dead.'

'Old Earth says sixty per cent casualties are acceptable,' Buzz said stepping into the crowd.

'Wouldn't matter if Port Mars said it was acceptable, Warrant Officer. Those losses are not acceptable to me,' Martel said, walking off.

'Start picking our people up, Buzz,' TJ said before he led Daniella to the GCR.

'Sure thing, TJ, I'll get this sorted out,' Buzz saluted before setting to work.

Salvage teams from the Fort Grey detachment and Fort Saturn roamed the battlefield collecting weapons of both sides and the bodies of all the dead.

*****

CHAPTER XIX
Tuesday, 10 April, 2251

The battle of Fort Saturn had been won. A weakness in the Bregan's strength had been found. Allies wandered in the southern forest waiting to be called upon. Now the armies of man could gather and strike this awesome threat and be rid of it.

The base commander for Fort Saturn knew all that but he also knew a victory in the field now would elevate him into the military ranks and out of this militia. The two squads that had joined the fight yesterday would be perfect to achieve his goals.

'I can't stay here anymore. These sometimes-soldiers couldn't even hold off a bunch of animals. If I can show the military command that they were the problem and that I can get things done, I could move into the city. First thing we need to do is get rid of their commander,' District Commander Shawn Norris said to his aide.

'Yes, sir,' she tapped the blue pad she held in one hand 'I'm setting up a transfer for Commander Martel to Port Mars.'

'Good, put it through immediately,' Commander Norris turned from his lavishly decorated office to gaze out the flex-steel window over the Fort Saturn dome. Perfectly smooth curve gave crystal definition to the silvery reflections dancing over the surface. The lack of clouds and a lighter than normal haze gave him the unique vision of there being four stars before him. This was going to be a great day to start his march out of here.

'Sir, Port Mars is requesting a second transfer for special assignment,' the aide stopped her red nails for a moment.

'Fine, fine,' he said without turning, 'Send a senior NCO from that Fort Grey lot. That should make it seem like we're not playing favourites.'

'Shall I assign a squad leader?'

'No, I am going to need the leadership to remain intact. Any of the others will do fine.'

'Yes, sir,' she said and set back to work.

'When you're done with that, send up a squad Captain. I want to get a strike plan together before the end of my shift.'

'Yes sir.' The aide turned and started for the door without looking up from her pad. As she reached the door she looked up and closed the door behind her all without losing a stride.

Commander Norris did not have to wait long before Captain Sarnet knocked at the door. He took a last look out over his city's dome then called for the officer to enter before moving to the planning table across the fifty-foot long office. The table was mixture of light, common wood and dark, rich grain either of which was a luxury in the colony compared to the usual cold metal. Captain Sarnet looked exhausted but still strode confidently as she walked up to the table, staying on the opposite side from the Commander. She set a dog-eared note pad on the table and leaned forward to listen to her new orders.

'As you can see here we have a pretty good lay of the land to the east of us,' Commander Norris proudly flaunted the 3D-engraved map of the Eden Peninsula embedded on the table top and under a glass plate. 'This is a hand carved representation of our colony as it was intended back in the terraforming days. I had the Comb Plateau added to keep up with the changes since then.'

'Impressive,' Captain Sarnet replied. She was soft spoken but always to the point.

'Yes, it is, isn't it,' he said, pleased with himself and his toy. It was only then he noticed the Captain's crumbled uniform. The grey utility pockets were torn from the mud spattered grey pants leg. Her dark red tunic was equally wrinkled and opened at the front as if it had been put on as she knocked at his door.

'You're a disgrace, Captain,' he commented almost matter-of-factly. 'When we are done here you will make yourself look like you actually give a damn about this city.'

'Sir, I was on recovery duty on the battlefield. Every trooper in the detachment was and is out there cleaning up and getting our dead back.'

'Enough excuses. See here,' Commander Norris indicated the rolling hills and green fields east of the Plateau. 'This terrain is easy travel in every direction. We will get out some people to the Miles Research Station for resupply by the end of the first day.'

'Sir, we haven't heard from MRS in over a month,' the Captain still made notes but shook her head.

'Search patterns will be laid out the following morning.' He did not break to even acknowledge she had spoken. 'We know those things fled east after the fight and Martel says he was attacked from the north. They have to be out there on the east coast. Since we haven't heard from New Venus in a while we can assume that those animals have not gotten that far north.'

'We don't know that, sir. The troopers from Fort Grey say that the Bregan can block transmissions as well as hear them. If we go by this twenty-year out of date map we're just asking for trouble. We don't know what's out there beyond the shipping route to the crystal fields.'

'Bah, ground is ground and animals are animals, Captain. Heck, we may even find that MRS has developed a little surprise for them.'

'This is just insane! I won't be a part of this. You're leading us straight at those monsters and you're data hasn't been verified in over two decades! I won't let anyone from this base go out there to die.' The erstwhile captain grabbed her pad and stormed off for the door.

'That's fine, Captain. I'll use the squads from Fort Grey then.' The Commander did not look up from his magical map.

'What? After all those people went through, you are just going send them out there? Their Major is still in critical condition!'

'That will be all, Captain.' Commander Norris finally looked up and walked towards the door savouring the sound of his own crisply pressed pants swishing as he moved. It was such a relief after enduring the Captain's disorder. The military would never let that fly. He stepped to the door and forced the Captain to back up and out of the office.

'Cathy,' he waved at his aide before returning to the perfection of his office.

The aide came into the room shortly after and closed the heavy door behind her. She glided to the side of his desk and awaited the Commander's dictation. Shawn loved her obedience and loyalty. It was going to be a shame to leave her behind when his promotion came.

'First, we need to get some promotions to those Fort Grey people to keep them happy. Make up some reason but make it sound realistic. Let get one of the Lieutenants and a couple of the non-commissioned troopers. Oh and a rookie! People love it when a rookie gets promoted. Make it some hard luck case.'

'Yes, sir,' she tapped away furiously.

'I'm going to need a speech too. See what you can come up with in the next little while. I want to go through it to correct any of your errors before I present it.'

He waved her off.

She turned and left without a word but still working at her note pad. After leaving the office she closed the door and let her arms drop with exhaustion. There was no way she could keep this up much longer. As she tossed her pad on to the desk, a trooper came into her own office. The dark grey combat jumpsuit indicated that this one was from the Fort Grey group but she knew this trooper well from the smell. The trooper had been marked as *trusted* by the new masters of Mars.

'I need to see Commander Norris,' the trooper said.

'I've got him handled like we discussed.' She moved closer. There was some animal attraction that came with being marked, especially from the newly chosen.

'This is serious. We need to talk about a deal.'

'There will be no deal today. Norris is sending squads out there to MRS in the next couple days. I overheard him talking it over with the detachment lead Captain,' She turned and went back to her desk. 'You'll just have to wait to get the deal done.'

When she turned back the trooper had left.

Quick and quiet, like her masters. She sat heavily into her chair and began working on the items for the Commander. An odd job here or there was not so bad before the new leaders of Eden show their strength.

*****